IN WILDCAT HOLLOW

THE HOLLOW AND THE COVE BOOK 1

ARI D.

Pisteuo Publications

Pisteuo Publications

1805 Sunset Drive

Marble Falls, TX 78654

Website: aridauthor.com

www.instagram.com/ari.d.author/

www.facebook.com/ari.d.author

CONTENTS

DEDICATION

In loving memory of Leona Brenner Rozell,
Who is watching her story be told from the finest seat in Heaven.

For those who have lost the memories of their childhood,
Who have forgotten the innocence of childhood,
Who didn't get the childhood they deserved,
And those who wish to make the best of their remaining childhood.

ONE

THE GUESTS AND THE KITTEN
AUGUST 1933

In the middle of a great, yellow meadow, near the town of Beaty, Arkansas, an ancient oak tree stood proud and tall. Its large limbs stretched out to provide shelter for any traveling bird and shade for any weary beast.

Three weathered boards had been leaned against the trunk of this oak tree to make a sort of rickety teepee or playhouse. The playhouse was repulsive to the eye of every passerby on the near dirt road, but it was a precious treasure to four little girls.

Twelve yards away from the oak tree stood a one-room log cabin, nestled between the cotton field and the woods. Inside was a busy Mama, singing as she washed the dishes to ready the house for company. She paused for a moment, brushing her caramel-colored hair out of her face. She smiled through the soiled window panes at her four daughters, who were playing near the oak tree.

Her oldest daughter was Clementine, nicknamed Mae. She was eight-years-old and enjoyed helping Mama with the cooking and cleaning. Daddy sometimes called her "Mama number two" which made everyone laugh, but it was true. Her deep blue eyes sparkled when she was deep in thought, and her vocabulary was extensive because of her constant reading.

Next was Louella, who they called Lou. She followed Daddy around the farm, planting the crops and taking care of their animals. Her favorite thing was to help Daddy take care of Daisy, their milk cow. Daddy alarmed Daisy, but Lou knew how to calm her down by petting her nose and whispering to her. Lou had black hair like her Daddy; she was the only one with this trait.

Chrissa was the third oldest. She didn't like her nicknames, but sometimes Daddy called her "Issa" to tease her. She had turned four on August first, and she now thought that she would start school later that month. Mama had told her otherwise, but that didn't dampen her hopes. She always wore pink dresses and pink ribbons, which highlighted her large brown eyes and freckles.

Mollyann, or Ann, as everyone called her, was the youngest. At two-years-old, she was very curious about the world. But she was also stubborn, and she didn't like it when her older sisters tried to boss her around. Daddy said that her hazel eyes, rimmed with green, reminded him of the cotton field outside.

The four girls were the daughters of the Moore family. They lived with their Mama, Amerie, their Daddy, Isam, and Missy. Missy was their border collie who guarded the house and helped Daddy hunt. She was very protective of the four girls and rarely let them out of her sight.

On this summer day, Missy was lying on the front porch with her eyes on the girls playing near the oak tree. Six-year-old Lou was lounging on a low tree branch while her younger sister, Chrissa, collected the fallen leaves. She was creating plates for her pretend food to sit on.

"Why are you putting the leaves on the ground?" Lou asked, leaning over the branch. "Put them on the table."

"But I don't have a table," Chrissa mumbled. "You're sitting on it."

Lou ignored the remark and sat up, extending her hand. "Mae, hand me the cup so I can wash it."

Ann had been using the porcelain cup to dig in the dirt, but was now throwing leaves into the air and watching them float away with fascination only a toddler could have.

Eight-year-old Mae thought of refusing Lou's demand, but she didn't want to cause a fight. She sat her cloth doll at the base of the tree and grabbed the cup. As she walked to hand the cup to Lou, however, she tripped over Ann. Ann cried out in surprise as the cup fell to the ground.

"Mae, look what you did to our only cup. Now it's broken," Lou moaned. She jumped down from the tree to examine the crack in the cup.

Mae dusted Ann's dress off as she grumbled, "Lou, you're the one who told me to hand you the cup."

"But you needed to be *careful* with it," Lou said, cradling the precious cup.

Mae huffed, shaking her head as she returned to her doll. Chrissa joined her, using a stick in place of her cloth doll, which was inside the house. Lou, still holding the cup, collapsed onto the ground.

A grasshopper hopped onto Ann's foot, and she screamed. Kicking her foot, it sailed into the air and landed on Mae's head.

"Oh, Ann, it was just a grasshopper," Lou chided. Noticing the bug crawling on Mae's hair, she casually said, "And now it's on Mae's head."

Mae's eyes widened, and she began squealing, "Get it off! Get it off! Lou, help me get it off!"

"I can't see it," Lou shrugged.

"Don't lie. You *can* see it, Louella!"

"It's blended into your hair." Lou threw her hands up in defeat.

Mae shook her braids and danced around until the bug fell onto the ground. She kicked it towards the tree and glared at Lou, panting from the excitement of the scare.

"You didn't even try to help me," Mae accused.

"It's yellow like your hair," Lou said, trying to hide a snicker behind her hand. "I couldn't see it."

Mae's eyes lit with rage, knowing Lou had intentionally *not* helped. Mae immediately began searching the ground for the poor grasshopper.

Chrissa put her arm around Ann and glared at Lou, who was still giggling. "Ann and me are going inside, Mae."

The girls walked to the house as Mae found the grasshopper again. Lou wasn't looking when Mae tossed the grasshopper at her. Lou screamed and ran behind the oak tree as Mae laughed. Lou returned, furious, and grabbed a handful of dirt. She threw it at Mae, who tried to shield her head from the dust that rained down.

"You're gonna get whooped if you don't quit being mean, Lou," Mae said as she dusted the dirt off of her dress and braids. "Mama said you have to be nice for the company tonight."

"I'm always nice for the company," Lou said, tossing her black hair behind her shoulder.

Chrissa ran to them from the house and said, "Mama wants you both to finish your chores."

The three girls sprinted to the house where Mama was stirring the big soup pot. The savory aroma filled the house and made the girls' mouths water. She turned and smiled at them, giving her instructions.

"Mae, finish washing the dishes and prepare the table for supper tonight. Lou, sweep the floor and empty the dirt outside. Chrissa, make the bed. When you are done, take Missy outside so she doesn't cause a ruckus when the guests arrive."

"Yes, Mama," the girls said.

After making the bed, Chrissa, Missy, and Ann went outside. Missy ran around the meadow, trying to catch grasshoppers in her mouth while Chrissa sat on the porch, dangling her feet over the edge. The tall grass tickled her bare feet.

Ann wandered to the other side of the porch, singing softly to herself some tune only known by her. She climbed off the porch, unnoticed by Chrissa. She was beginning to walk towards the cotton field, where she had seen Daddy working, when a soft meow caught her attention. Bending over to look underneath the porch, she came face to face with a fuzzy gray kitten, curled in a ball a few feet away. Ann's curious hazel eyes locked with the kitten's soft green eyes. Another quiet meow escaped the kitten.

"Puppy," Ann said, pointing.

Chrissa didn't look up.

"Puppy," Ann said again, then giggled.

"Missy's not over there," Chrissa said, glancing towards Ann.

"Puppy," Ann said, more firmly.

Chrissa rolled off the edge of the porch. "Ann, there's no pup-" She stopped short, then squealed. The startled kitten fled to the other end of the porch and pressed itself against the house. Ann cried out in distress.

"Lou! Mae! Hurry!" Chrissa yelled.

The girls raced out of the house. Lou still held the broom, and Mae's hands were dripping with dirty dishwater.

"What is it?" Mae asked.

"Puppy," Ann said, pointing underneath the porch.

"It's a kitten," Chrissa corrected.

Lou's eyes grew wide. "Really?"

Chrissa and Ann nodded their heads.

"Oh! I can catch it! Give me just one minute," Lou squealed, dashing inside the house to finish sweeping. A minute later she ran back out, panting, and squirmed underneath the porch.

"Yes. Come here, kitty," Lou coaxed. "No, not over *there!*"

"What are y'all doing?" Daddy asked, scooping Chrissa and Ann into a big hug.

"There's a kitty under there," Chrissa said.

"Puppy," Ann insisted.

Another meow came from underneath the porch.

"Catch it, Lou!" Mae exclaimed.

There was a frustrated meow and Lou shouted, "Got it!" She

wiggling out from underneath the porch and stood up, cradling the furry gray ball.

"Aww," they all cooed, including Daddy.

"Mae, the dishes aren't-" Mama stopped, noticing the kitten in Lou's hand. She put her hand on her hip and sighed, smiling in spite of herself. "What are y'all doing?"

"Lou caught a kitten," Mae said as Lou held out the dark gray ball.

"Can we keep it?" Chrissa asked.

Mama looked from one face to another, the girls' and Daddy's, each one pleading for the kitten to stay. Her eyes finally rested on the kitten itself, so helpless on its own. She sighed, "Alright."

Everyone celebrated, and Mama smiled. They brought the kitten inside and laid some blankets in the corner of the kitchen for her. She shrank away from the girls' prodding hands, and Daddy finally told them to watch her from a distance. The subject of the kitten's name was introduced, and the arguing began.

"Her name needs to be Fluff," Lou said.

"No. Name it Baby," Ann demanded.

Lou tried again, "She looks like a little fluff ball."

"I like the name Fluff," Chrissa said.

"Her name should be CoCo," Mae said.

"Why would we name her CoCo?" Lou ridiculed.

Mae examined the kitten. "She looks like Mama's hot cocoa."

Chrissa, Lou, and Daddy studied the kitten.

"She does," Chrissa breathed.

"I like CoCo," Daddy said.

"Let's name her CoCo," Lou said as if she'd thought of the name herself.

The company expected for dinner was forgotten until Missy began barking. Mama gasped and hurried around the kitchen to finish the soup. The girls ran out of the house in a whirlwind and raced to be the first to meet the guests.

The guests were their neighbors, the Alexanders. The Alexanders had one daughter, Frances, and one son, Clarence. Frances was eight-years-old, like Mae, but Clarence was a baby. All four girls loved playing with Frances because of her imagination. She could turn any boring situation into a wild adventure.

Frances stepped out of the wagon and was surrounded by the four Moore girls. They grabbed her hands and practically dragged her into the house in their anticipation to show her CoCo. The five girls cooed over the tiny kitten, not daring to pet her because of Daddy's warning.

Mr. and Mrs. Alexander climbed out of the wagon slower, carrying baby Clarence with them. Mama and Daddy greeted their guests a little more civilized than the girls, but Daddy was no less excited to show them CoCo. Mr. and Mrs. Alexander were led into the house and properly introduced to the kitten.

After dinner, the girls were disappointed to find that CoCo had taken refuge underneath the girls' bed. Try as they might, they could not reach her. Mama instructed them to go play outside. They reluctantly did so, and sat on the porch with Missy, swinging their feet over the edge.

"What do we play now?" Chrissa asked.

"We could try and catch grasshoppers with Missy. Look, Missy, grasshopper," Lou said, pointing into the meadow.

Missy launched off of the porch and ran through the meadow. Hundreds of grasshoppers flew up in her wake, squeaking their disapproval at the intruder. Missy jumped up to catch them in her mouth, making the girls giggle.

Frances said, "We could play restaurant."

"What is a restaurant?" Chrissa asked.

"It's a fancy place to eat," Mae said.

"One time my parents took me to eat at one," Frances said.

"Aw, lucky!" Lou said.

"We can't even get soda pop at the gas station," Chrissa said. "Mama says it costs too much."

"But it's only a nickel," Frances frowned.

"Was the restaurant good?" Lou asked.

"Yeah, and my parents said they'd take me again soon." Frances said.

Mae shrugged. "I've only read about restaurants in books."

"Let's play it, then," Lou said, jumping up.

They ran to the playhouse by the oak tree and CoCo was quickly forgotten. The evening passed all too quickly, and before the girls knew it, the Alexanders were pulling away in their buggy. The girls were told to dress for bed and say their prayers.

"I pray that we will all sleep well," Mae said.

"I pray for CoCo, and that she will not be scared of us anymore," Lou prayed.

Chrissa bowed her head. "I pray that I will start school this year."

Ann was too young to understand prayer, but Daddy clasped her hands between his and said, "We pray for Your protection through the night and for Your blessing upon our family. Amen."

The girls opened their eyes and climbed into the bed they shared, which was a pallet of blankets on the floor that was rolled up during the day. After they were tucked in and kissed goodnight by Daddy, Mama sang them one of her favorite songs, *Come and Dine,* until they fell asleep.

Jesus has a table spread
where the saints of God are fed.
He invites His chosen people, 'Come and dine.'
With His manna He doth feed
and supplies our every need:
oh, 'tis sweet to sup with Jesus all the time!
'Come and dine,' the Master calleth,
'Come and dine.' You may feast at Jesus' table all the time;
He who fed the multitude, turned the water into wine,
to the hungry calleth now, 'Come and dine.'

TWO

POPCORN AND FIREFLIES
SEPTEMBER 1933

"Lou! LEAVE THE KITTEN ALONE!" Mae cried.

"But CoCo has Charlotte!" Lou argued.

CoCo ran around the rocker in the living room, Lou right on her tail.

"Drop the doll, CoCo," Chrissa demanded, sounding less threatening than she intended.

CoCo ignored her and raced around the table.

"Leave her alone, Lou," Mama said, putting her hands on her hips as she watched the chaos.

"But Charlotte!" Lou cried, lunging towards the kitten again.

CoCo dodged the attack and took refuge underneath the girls' bed. Lou cried out again and stuck her arm underneath the bed to reach the doll.

"This is what happens when you have a cat," Mama said, shaking her head as she returned to the supper dishes she was washing.

"Please get my doll out," Lou said.

"I'll help," Mae told Mama.

Chrissa was hanging off of the bed trying to find CoCo, and Lou was collapsed on the floor trying to find Charlotte.

"You have to be gentle with the kitten," Mae chided, sliding to her knees by the bed. "Come, kitty. Come here, CoCo," she coaxed, and soon enough, CoCo left her hiding place, carrying the doll with her.

Lou snatched Charlotte away from CoCo. CoCo jumped onto the windowsill and stretched out to take a nap. The sun was about to disappear behind the cotton fields, and its golden rays filtered through the open window as if the light was solid. The birds chirped their goodnights to each other, the sound drifting into the house by the soft wind.

"Lou, next time put away Charlotte when you're done playing with her," Mae said, getting off the floor.

"It wasn't my fault. It was Ann's," Lou argued, hugging her doll. "She wanted to play with a doll and *you* wouldn't let her play with yours, so I had to let her play with mine."

"Not true," Mae said.

"Is so," Lou said, standing up and lifting her chin as if to challenge Mae.

"Hey, now," Mama said, and the girls knew to quit arguing.

"Where is Ann?" Chrissa asked.

Mae looked out the front door, spotting Ann and Missy on the edge of the porch. "Outside," she called over her shoulder before skipping over to play with Ann.

"Wait for me," Lou said, shoving Charlotte underneath the bed quilt and flying outside to join them.

"What are you doing, Ann?" Mae was asking her when Lou walked outside.

"Shhh. Watch," Ann said, putting her finger on her lips and looking out towards the meadow.

Missy sat still and alert, watching the meadow for any signs of life. Mae and Lou sat down beside her. They made not a sound as they watched for whatever Ann had seen.

There was a small blink of light near the oak tree.

Ann gasped, pointing, but the light was already gone. "What is it?"

"It's a firefly, Ann," Mae said. "They come out at night and -"

"There's another one!" Lou exclaimed, pointing.

"A what?" Chrissa asked, joining them.

"A firefly," Lou said.

"A bug!" Chrissa shrieked, taking a step back and throwing her arms in front of her face.

"It's a nice bug, Chrissa. It doesn't bite," Mae said.

"There it is again," Lou said, jumping up. "I'm gonna catch it."

"Don't hurt it," Ann said.

Lou raced down the porch stairs and out into the meadow where they had last sighted the firefly. She chased the small flicker of light. When it blinked out, she waved her arms blindly in the air. She stopped, breathing hard, before another light popped on.

"Catch it, Lou! Catch it!" Mae cried as she stood up. She raced down the stairs with Ann at her heels and clasped the air around her for a firefly. Missy followed, jumping into the air in pursuit of any flying creature. Giggles and shrieks of laughter echoed through the meadow and around the little house.

Mama smiled, watching the girls play as she leaned against the doorframe.

Daddy walked up behind her and smiled, "What are they doing?"

"Trying to catch fireflies," Mama said.

Daddy's eyes lit up. "I'll help." He bounded down the porch steps and joined the girls in the meadow.

"Help us catch a firefly, Daddy," Mae said.

"You have to be still and wait for them to fly near you," Daddy chided, and Mae stopped waving her hands around in the air. Mae and Ann stood still and waited for a bug to light up near them.

A small glow of light lit Mae's face up. She gasped and cupped her hands around it. She then peaked into the cracks between her fingers to see if she had caught it.

"Did you catch one?" Daddy asked.

"Look," Mae whispered into her hands. She showed Daddy the bug while Ann grasped at her elbow.

"I want to see," Ann said.

Mae lowered her hands so that Ann could see into them.

Ann put her eye in the small crack between Mae's fingers and waited breathlessly. After a moment, there was a tiny spark. Ann gasped and backed away from Mae's hand before coming right back to it to watch the little bug light up again.

Lou joined them and looked into Mae's hands. "Wow," she sighed.

Daddy laughed at their delight. "You know, if you let the firefly go, it will grant you a wish."

"Really?" Mae asked.

"Really," Daddy said. "Go on, make your wish, and then open your hand."

Mae squeezed her eyes shut. "I wish that my life will always be like this, and that Mama and Daddy will always be here, and that we will live in this house forever."

She looked up at Daddy, who smiled. She hesitantly opened her hand while Lou and Ann watched. The little bug sat in her palm for a moment, as if to say thank you, before flying off. It blinked a goodbye as it disappeared into the night sky.

"I'm gonna catch one," Lou said, skipping away.

"Me too," Ann said.

The girls raced around the meadow again, clasping the air for fireflies.

"You have to be *still*," Daddy laughed.

"I see it! It's above me! Oh, can't reach it!" Lou said, jumping in the air.

Mae stood quietly and watched the dark sky for another blink of light. Ann gave up trying to find a firefly and collapsed onto the grass, watching Lou jump around. Mama was inside, cooking something that smelled delicious while Chrissa sat on the porch, watching with a mixture of interest and fear.

"You gonna join us, Chrissa?" Daddy asked.

Chrissa tilted her head. "Well..."

Lou screamed, "I caught one!"

"Hold on, Lou, or you'll smash it," Daddy said, laughing as he ran to her side.

"Make your wish, Lou," Mae said.

"I wish..." she thought for a minute. "That Ann will get her own doll for Christmas so that I don't have to share mine no more."

Daddy laughed.

Mae gasped, "Look!"

A firefly was crawling on her hand, lighting up every few seconds.

"Do you want this wish, Ann?" Mae asked.

Ann nodded her head.

"Go ahead," Mae urged.

"I wish for another cup for the playhouse," Ann said.

Mae smiled and released the firefly.

Chrissa joined them in the meadow and began grasping for fireflies, rather hesitantly.

"I caught two," Daddy said, showing the girls.

"That must mean twice good luck," Mae said.

A firefly landed on Chrissa's forehead, and she screamed.

"It's okay, Chrissa. Look, I caught another one, but you can have the wish," Lou said, holding out her hand.

Chrissa shrank away from the extended hand, but accepted the wish. "I wish for more ribbons."

Lou laughed as she released the firefly.

"It's for when I have two braids," Chrissa pouted.

Mama brought popcorn outside on the porch in two large bowls.

"So *that's* what smelled so good!" Daddy exclaimed.

"Race you there," Lou said, running through the meadow. Mae followed in hot pursuit. Daddy grabbed Chrissa and Ann, placing one under each arm as he ran to the porch. They all fell in a cluster of giggles at Mama's feet.

The popcorn was deliciously salted and the perfect snack for an evening like this. The girls ate it slowly, watching the fireflies gather and light up the meadow. Missy was still trying to catch the fireflies in her mouth, to the girls' amusement.

When the popcorn was gone, the girls ran back into the yard where more fireflies had gathered than before. They spent the rest of the evening catching fireflies and making wishes as Mama and Daddy watched from the porch, smiling with delight at their four little girls.

THREE

CHRISTMAS AND ANN'S DOLL

"Lou! Mae! Wake up, it's Christmas!" Chrissa yelled.

"Wha-" Lou blinked, the squealed, "Christmas!" She threw back the blankets and sprung from the bed.

"Merry Christmas, girls," Mama said from the rocking chair where CoCo purred on her lap.

"Merry Christmas, Mama," Chrissa and Lou said.

Mae sat up, half asleep, and rubbed her eyes.

Ann climbed off the bed and stumbled on the cold floor towards the Christmas tree. She didn't know what was going on because this was only her second Christmas. Chrissa and Lou found their gifts and then helped Ann find hers.

The Christmas tree was a pine tree Daddy had chopped down from the forest nearby. He nailed two pieces of wood at the bottom in the shape of a cross so that it would stand up. The tip of it nearly touched the ceiling of the tiny cabin. Daddy placed it in a corner of the living room so that it could be seen from everywhere in the house.

The girls decorated it with strings of popped corn, paper snowflakes, and glass balls from Mae's first Christmas. Daddy carved a star out of some wet firewood and placed it on top. With the star, it did scrape the ceiling.

The mantle was decorated with Mama's ornately carved nativity set. Daddy had carved it for her during their first Christmas together. It was one of Mama's most treasured items.

The door opened and Daddy walked in with a stack of wood. "Merry Christmas, girls," he said, placing the wood near the fireplace.

Ann toddled towards him, and he scooped her into his bear hug.

"Merry Christmas, Daddy," the girls chorused.

Mae joined the group at the Christmas tree. There were two presents for each daughter. They knew one of their presents was a homemade dress, but they didn't know what the other was. Daddy sat beside Mama's rocking chair, and they looked on, smiling, as the girls opened their presents.

Mae received a beautiful purple dress with white lace trim around the edges. She fingered the lace lovingly, her blue eyes sparkling with delight as she examined the dress. Her second gift was a white beaded necklace, which she promptly put on over her night-gown. The other girls couldn't take their eyes off of it for three whole minutes, fingering it and gasping with delight at its beauty.

Lou was thrilled when she opened her lovely pale green dress. It was pretty, but not too pretty, as she liked to say. Mama had sewn four large white buttons down the front as decoration, and Ann was confused why they wouldn't open.

"It's fake, Ann," Lou said.

"Fake?" Ann asked, not knowing the word.

"It's pretend," Mae said.

Ann nodded her head slowly, "Oh."

Lou's second present was a notebook and a small box of pencils.

"You'll need those to start school next year," Mama said.

Lou shrugged, not particularly excited to think about starting school. She got up and hugged Mama anyway because she wasn't ungrateful for the gift.

Chrissa squealed when she opened her new pink dress and lace shawl. She held it up to her shoulders and spun, watching the bottom twirl as she giggled. She also got a toy top, which she began spinning on the floor. Daddy had carved it from leftover firewood and had engraved swirly designs into the sides.

Ann needed help unwrapping her presents since she was still young. She got a pretty red dress and a beautiful cloth doll. It had light brown eyes and a small smile stitched onto the face. Its dress was made of strips of cloth that were leftover from the girls' new dresses and Mama's quilting. Braided strips of cloth stuck out of each side, tied at the ends to look like puffy sleeves.

Ann traced the doll's face lovingly and examined the strips of cloth with awe. Mama smiled from the rocker as Ann clutched the doll excitedly and refused to put it down.

After careful questioning, her older sisters found that Ann had named her doll Cobweb Windowlight.

"Why would you name it Cobweb, Ann?" Lou asked.

"Cobweb *Windowlight*," Ann corrected.

"That's almost worse," Lou groaned.

"Ann, don't you want to name it something pretty?" Mae asked. "Mine's name is Lolly, Ann. Don't you like that name?"

"Mine's named Rachel," Chrissa said, stroking her doll's head.

"My doll's name is Charlotte. I think Charlotte is a good name for a doll," Lou said, jumping towards the bed to grab her doll.

"Girls, leave Ann alone. I think Cobweb Windowlight is a great name for a doll," Mama said.

"Cobweb sounds like a good name for a pet spider," Lou volunteered, and Daddy laughed.

Mama announced it was breakfast time. She pushed CoCo off her lap and grunted as she climbed out of the rocking chair. Ann noticed her tummy was sticking out more than usual but shrugged it off.

Daddy added a log to the dying fire to heat the house. Mama

scrambled some eggs and made toast while Mae took down the honey and butter from the cabinets. The younger girls squealed when they saw the coveted treats.

Christmas breakfast was just as wonderful as could be. The food was savored by all seated around the table. Missy, who was seated *underneath* the table, enjoyed their breakfast too. The joy of Christmas hung in the air like fog over a lake early in the morning.

When breakfast was over, Daddy said, "We will be joining the Alexanders for Christmas dinner at noon, so you girls need to put on your new dresses after breakfast is cleaned up."

The girls squealed with delight until Mama's stern look calmed them down at the table.

"May I help you make the gingerbread, Mama?" Mae asked.

"She only wants to help you because then she can lick the spoon," Lou complained.

"Not true," Mae said.

"Lou, don't make assumptions unless you're willing to make the gingerbread," Mama scolded, picking up the breakfast dishes. "Of course you can help, Mae."

Right after the dishes were washed and the rest of breakfast put away, Mae and Mama began mixing the gingerbread dough. Daddy brought the ham out of the smokehouse and began slicing it. Chrissa and Ann played with their dolls near the fireplace. Lou slid into the kitchen and hung around the table, waiting for the mixing bowl to be retired so that she could lick it.

"You can help us, Lou," Mama said with a grin. "I need someone to wash the dishes, mix the batter, and put the pans in the oven."

Lou realized there was more work in the job than she was willing to trade for a lick of gingerbread dough. "I think I'll just go play with Ann and Chrissa."

"That's what I thought," Mama laughed.

When the gingerbread came out of the brick oven, the wonderful scent drifted throughout the house and made the girls' stomachs growl.

"Can we *please* try a piece?" Lou begged.

"Just one tiny piece?" Chrissa said.

Mama shook her head. "You can have one after dinner."

After the gingerbread had cooled and the ham prepared, Daddy loaded all the girls into the wagon and covered them with warm blankets that had hung near the fireplace. The blankets warmed the girls at the beginning of the trip, but they were shivering from the wind by the time they reached the Alexander's house.

Mrs. Alexander opened the door, hurrying the Moores into her cozy house. They stomped the snow off of their boots as best they could before they entered. The gingerbread cookies were cold, but Mama put them on the mantle of the fireplace to warm them back up.

The girls shed their coats and mittens at the door while Frances rushed to her bed to grab her new porcelain doll. They gasped when Frances showed them her doll. It had a shiny white face with red lips and beautiful green eyes like Frances'. Its hair was curly, golden locks that reached her shoulders. Its dress was made of light pink cloth, and its shoes were made of real leather.

All five girls retreated into a corner of the house, admiring the doll.

"She's beautiful, Frances," Mae said, stroking the doll's soft hair.

Chrissa sighed, "I wish I had one."

Mae jabbed her in the ribs, causing Chrissa to screech. Frances didn't seem to notice.

"Her dress is pretty," Lou said as she rubbed the doll's dress between her fingers.

"Mine too," Ann said, pushing Cobweb Windowlight into the middle of the circle.

"I love her," Frances said to Ann.

Ann beamed in delight as she embraced Cobweb Windowlight.

Mrs. Alexander approached the little group and smiled down at them, "It's dinner time."

The girls shouted in their excitement, not for dinner, but for the delicious gingerbread they knew would be for dessert.

The two families huddled together in that little house, enjoying Christmas dinner and the friendship they had. Hearty laughs echoed around the house as jokes were told and tales were spun. And it truly was a merry Christmas.

FOUR

THE DEATH AND THE BIRTH

FEBRUARY 1934

"Ann! Keep away from your Daddy," Mama scolded.

Ann jumped away from the rocker, frightened by Mama's stern voice. She wanted to see why Daddy's legs were in a bucket, and why he'd been sitting in the chair for so long. She craned her neck to look into the bucket.

Daddy moaned quietly.

Ann yelped and flew to Mama's side. She decided she didn't want to know why. She didn't want to know why Daddy moaned during the night or why Mama seemed so tired and upset.

Mae stopped washing the breakfast dishes and frowned. Ann held up her hands to Mama, wanting to be picked up. Mama sat in a chair and pulled Ann on what little lap remained when she sat down. Ann grabbed a piece of Mama's hair and began toying with it as Mama stared solemnly off into the distance.

"Mama?"

"Yes, Mae?"

"Why is Daddy sitting and not getting up?"

Mama sighed, "He's sick. Very sick."

"With what?"

Ann slid off of Mama's lap and toddled to her bed to grab Cobweb Windowlight. She plopped onto the floor and began playing quietly with her doll while Mama answered.

"Doctor Watson doesn't know what it is. Daddy's legs keep filling up with fluid and draining into the bucket. The doctor doesn't know what to do." Mama's voice sounded choked.

Mae was silent for a minute. "Will he be okay?"

"The doctor doesn't know. He says it's nothing like he's ever seen before. I guess there's a possibility that Daddy ... is going to die." Mama put her head into her hands and sobbed.

Mae was startled. She didn't know how to respond. She turned back to the dirty dishes, desperately searching for something comforting to say to Mama.

Mama noticed Mae's concerned expression and wiped away a tear. "I'm sorry. I shouldn't be telling you this. You're too young to have to ... bear the weight."

"God will heal him," Mae said quickly, trying to stop Mama from crying.

Mama wiped away another tear. "Maybe."

"I know God will heal him because God can do anything," Mae said confidently, turning back to the breakfast dishes she was supposed to be washing.

"Maybe," Mama said again.

Ann was concerned that Mama was crying too. She stood up and ran to Mama, hugging her legs and saying "I'm sorry, Mama."

Mama smiled meekly, and Mae returned to the dirty dishes, confident in her statement that God would heal Daddy.

But, just like Mama feared, Daddy passed on to Heaven on February eleventh, nineteen thirty-four.

The girls found Mama weeping on the living room floor next to Daddy's rocker. Mae was the first to realize what had happened. She collapsed onto the floor and sobbed, hugging Mama. Chrissa leaned against Mama and cried. Lou ran out of the house, refusing to believe what had happened.

Ann walked up to Daddy and touched his cold hand. "Wake up, Daddy," she said softly.

When the mortician came to carry away Daddy's body in his old, broken-down wagon, Lou screamed. Collapsing on Mama's lap, she called Daddy's name over and over again until her voice was completely gone. Ann and the other girls huddled around Mama's chair, crying as they watched the wagon leave the little house.

The funeral was held at their church. It was freezing, even though there was a roaring fire in the stove. Sleet and snow fell from the sky, as if heaven itself was mourning with the little family. Ann shivered and huddled close to Mama during the long sermon.

The casket was black wood. It was closed, but Ann knew that her Daddy was hidden inside of it. There was a big American flag draped over it, nearly covering it, as if hiding the casket could hide the fact that Daddy was gone. Ann looked down the pew at Lou, Mae, and Chrissa. Silent tears trickled down their faces.

When they lowered the casket into the grave at the burial site, there was a gun salute. Seven shots were fired by three guns. Ann covered her ears and huddled closer to Mama. Mama held Ann close, her tears dripping onto Ann's hair.

Grandmother and Grandfather Bates came to visit right after the funeral. They were Mama's mother and step-father. They didn't want Mama to be alone with the girls and the farm work while she was *expecting*.

Grandmother had shaky hands, so she kept mostly to knitting tiny socks and caps. The girls didn't understand why she made these because 'they're much too small to fit Ann.' Mae and Lou helped Mama with the housework and making dinner. Grandfather cared for the fields and said many words the girls hadn't learned yet while he was at it.

There was much talk about where the family would go to make a living.

"It's not a good idea to leave you in this town to fend for yourself. You've got four little girls, another one expected any day, and no one to help you earn the money," Grandmother said one evening as she mended Grandfather's sock in front of the fire. "There's also housework to be done, and Mae and Lou can't do it all the time. Look at how tired they are."

She pointed at Lou, who was slumped over the table, asleep with the broom still in her hand.

"I don't need any help, Mother," Mama said, not taking her eyes off of the baby quilt she was making.

"I think otherwise," Grandmother said. "Of course, Grandfather Bates and I could always move down here with you."

"Oh, Mother, you can't move down here. You still have some years left to sharecrop for Boss Allen," Mama said.

"Boss Allen, pish-posh. He made it clear that we can leave whenever we need to," Grandmother assured her.

Mama shook her head. "Boss Allen won't let you move here."

"Well then, what if *you* come to *us*?" Grandmother asked.

Mama shook her head again. "That won't work."

"Why not?"

"The girls will be heartbroken to leave their friends. Frances and the Alexanders and-"

"I know you will all be sad to leave, but don't you want to be near family so that we can help? Being a single mother is hard. I know."

"But that was by choice."

"That's because your father is a-"

"Mother," Mama warned, glancing over to where Chrissa and Ann were playing dolls on their bed.

Grandmother scoffed, "Either way, I know how hard it is to be a single mother, and I don't want that burden to be placed on you."

"There are just … so many memories here," Mama said.

"I know, Amerie, but just wait and see. There can be new memories," Grandmother said, patting Mama's leg.

They spent a moment in silence.

Finally, Mama agreed to move up near Grandmother and Grandfather Bates.

"You can move in May when you and the baby are nice and healthy," Grandmother said. "That leaves us plenty of time to prepare a place for you to live."

Mama smiled a weak smile.

"It will be nice to have the children running around with their Aunt Loretta. I fear she gets mighty lonesome, up there on the farm with no children to play with. Such a shame she was born so many years later than her older siblings," Grandmother sighed, returning to her mending.

"Mama!" Mae yelled, running inside. "A letter for you from Uncle Roy."

"Roy?" Mama and Grandmother asked at the same time.

"Yes," Mae said, handing Mama the letter.

Mama tore it open and read through, giving a cry of relief when it was finished.

"Roy and Ester are coming next week!" Mama said, handing the letter to Grandmother.

Grandmother sighed, " Oh, that's wonderful!"

Grandmother and Grandfather Bates left one day before Uncle Roy and Aunt Ester arrived. Happy greetings were passed around the group as the four girls welcomed their two older cousins, Louis and Earl. The bags were unloaded and brought into the house before the adults sat in the living room to talk and the kids were sent outside to play.

On February twenty-fifth, three days after Uncle Roy and Aunt Ester came to help, Mama gave birth to a son, whom she named Jack Isam.

The girls were completely shocked when Jack was born. Mama hadn't mentioned being pregnant to them. They had noticed her body changed, but she hadn't said anything about it. When they first met Jack Isam, they squealed and jumped around for joy. Mama allowed them to pass him around, carefully. They awed over his tiny face and head full of black hair.

"Like his Daddy's," Mama choked, somewhere between a laugh and a cry.

Aunt Ester made sure Mama was resting and that the kids kept quiet while inside the house. While Mama rested, Uncle Roy did odd jobs around the community to earn some money for the little family.

Uncle Roy and Aunt Ester's sons, Louis and Earl, were trouble-makers. Their favorite thing to do was cause trouble on the farm. They spat on the girls, pestered Missy, and attacked CoCo with acorns. One day they took Cobweb Windowlight and threw her into the air between them.

"Give her back," Ann screamed, tears running down her face.

"Make us," Louis snarled.

"Give it back to her," Mae said, "or I'll make you."

The boys stopped tossing the doll and looked at Mae.

"You can't make us," Louis scoffed.

"Oh yeah? Just wait and see."

"Then come and get me," Earl tempted, waving the doll in the air.

Mae ran at Earl, who had not been expecting a chase. He shrieked and ran around the house, clutching the doll. Lou, who was sitting on a stump, fell off with laughter. After a few rounds around the house, Earl began slowing within Mae's grasp. Finally, he dropped the doll and ran to hide behind Louis, who scowled at Mae.

Mae nodded her head curtly and handed the sandy doll to Ann.

Earl scoffed. "I could'a out ran you."

"You didn't," Mae said, putting her hand on her hip.

"Now see here, girlie," Louis began, stepping forward.

Mae stepped under his nose, challenging his authority with as fierce a glare as his own.

"Boys, it's chore time," Uncle Roy called from the barn.

Louis glared at Mae for a second longer before turning to obey his father's instructions. Earl followed sheepishly.

Mae turned to Ann, who was dusting off the doll and wiping

away tears. "There you go Ann, but you must keep your doll in a safe place where the boys can't find it."

"I will, Mae," Ann said. She finished cleaning her doll and took refuge inside the house.

"That was funny," Lou said, picking herself up off the ground.

"That was *not* funny, and I don't like those boys," Mae said, crossing her arms and glaring at the barn.

"I like them," Lou said. "They always let me play soldiers with them or fish in the creek."

Mae continued to scowl.

"I don't like it when they're mean to CoCo or Missy, though," Lou said after a minute. "They can't be mean to my dog."

FIVE

THE MOVE AND ANN'S BIRTHDAY

"Lou! Get off the truck roof before you fall and break an arm," Mama yelled.

Lou, who had been laying in the sun on top of Mr. Smith's truck, jerked her head up and found Mama on the front porch. She reluctantly climbed off of Mr. Smith's truck as Mama nodded her head and walked back inside the house.

Mr. Smith had volunteered to drive the Moore family to Grandfather and Grandmother Bates' house in his small pickup truck. Boss Allen's property was in Newark, Arkansas, near the White and Black Rivers.

It had been arranged for Mama and her kids to sharecrop for Boss Allen in exchange for a house to live in. When Mama and the kids sharecropped, they picked Boss Allen's cotton for a share of the profit. They were to make the hundred-mile trip the following morning at dawn.

"Mae, aren't you excited to move closer to Grandmother and Grandfather Bates?" Lou asked, finding Mae in the oak tree in the middle of the meadow.

Mae frowned, looking down at two-year-old Ann who was

playing in the playhouse. "I'm not sure. I think it will be lovely to move closer to our cousins, but I don't want to move away from Frances and my other friends."

"But it will be fun, won't it, Ann?"

"Fun," Ann repeated.

Mae didn't look convinced.

"Besides, we get to ride in Mr. Smith's truck," Lou said, glancing at the truck with excitement.

"Is Daisy riding in the truck with us?" Ann asked.

"No, Daisy is staying with Mr. Smith," Lou reminded her.

Ann stuck her bottom lip out. "I want Daisy to come with us."

"Me too. But she'll be okay with Mr. Smith," Lou said.

Mae shrugged, "What about CoCo?"

"Mama says she can take care of herself," Lou said.

"But I don't want to leave her here," Mae said, her eyes beginning to pool with tears.

"Mama said CoCo will get lost if she comes with us," Lou said.

Mae sniffed and looked away from Lou, wiping her tears. "I just don't want to leave her here," she repeated softly.

"Girls, come inside and have some supper," Mama called, peeking her head out of the door. Lou raced Ann to the house while Mae trudged along behind them.

The house was bare now. Grandmother and Grandfather Bates had sent their wagon to retrieve most of the furniture so that it would arrive before Mama and the kids. Only the stove and cabinets remained in the little house. A few blankets and pillows thrown around the room made up their sleeping arrangements for the evening. The table and chairs were gone, so they ate on the floor around a pot of soup.

Morning came all too quickly and soon they were jostling along the dirt roads in Mr. Smith's truck. Mama sat in the cab with the two youngest, Jack and Ann. Ann protested because she wanted to ride in the bed of the truck with the older girls, but Mama refused to let her ride back there for fear she'd fall out. Missy sat in the the bed of the truck with the older girls and stuck her head out the side, tongue flapping in the wind.

They traveled like this for three days. On the third day, they topped a tall hill and saw Grandmother and Grandfather Bates' house nestled at the bottom. Everyone cheered and shouted for joy; the long trip was finally over.

When they stopped at the bottom of the hill, all four Moore girls tumbled out of the truck and chased each other around the yard. Grandmother and Grandfather Bates walked outside and were attacked with hugs. Mama's half-sister, Loretta, came outside when Grandmother beckoned. She stayed close to the door, however.

When the adult's conversation became too boring for her, Lou asked Loretta, "Who are you?"

"Lou! Don't be rude," Mae scolded, jabbing Lou with her elbow.

Lou yelped and glared at Mae.

"Girls, this is your aunt Loretta," Grandmother said. "Don't you remember her?"

"No," Lou said flatly.

"We must have been too little to remember," Mae said, scowling at Lou.

"She's too young to be an aunt," Chrissa said, squinting against the sun.

Grandmother laughed, "She's your Mama's youngest sister, so she is younger than your other uncles and aunts."

"Why didn't you come with Grandmother and Grandfather Bates before Jack was born?" Lou asked.

"I stayed with a friend so I could continue my schooling," Loretta replied with an air of arrogance.

"Well," Mama said, "Should we take a look at our new house?"

The girls squealed and climbed back into the truck. Grandmother, Grandfather, and Loretta climbed in beside them, and the truck lurched forward. It was only half a mile to the Moore's new house, but the lurching and jolting of the old truck on the worn dirt roads made the trip seem longer.

The new house was a quaint, one-room log cabin. It was nestled between two tall cotton fields and the dirt road that ran within Boss Allen's property. The house was only a quarter of a mile away from the White River, and the girls could easily spot it's winding neck from the back porch.

Inside, there was a tiny stove and a fireplace in opposite corners, two doors, on opposite walls, and four windows, one for each wall. Other than the stove and fireplace, there was no furniture inside the house. Mama was able to squeeze the two beds, cabinets, a table, and chairs into the house before running out of room.

The flag that had laid on Daddy's casket was unfolded and neatly draped along the wall behind the beds. Mama stood for a moment and looked at it lovingly. Mae ran to the house and stopped short at the door. A soulful moment, Mama turned around.

"Mr. Smith is about to leave," Mae said.

Mama walked outside. "Leaving so soon?"

Mr. Smith closed the bed of his truck and nodded. "Gotta get back home."

Mama smiled. "Tell the Alexanders I said hi."

"I will," Mr. Smith promised as he climbed into his truck.

The next week was spent in preparation for Ann's third birthday, which was on the eighteenth of May. On that day, everyone would gather at Grandmother and Grandfather's house for supper and cake. Mama's two younger sisters, Amy and Mabel, would join them with their families.

Mama had not seen Aunt Mabel since she'd last visited Grandmother Bates' house two years prior. She'd last seen Aunt Amy four years earlier when Aunt Amy had moved away with her husband, George, who was in the navy. But George had been discharged from the navy after an accident, so they now lived in Newark, Arkansas with Grandmother Bates and Aunt Mabel.

On Ann's birthday, Mama and the kids went to Grandmother Bates' house during the early afternoon to prepare the cake and supper. Loretta and Mae sat in the living room, knitting, while the other kids were playing outside.

Ann pushed a chair up to the counter and, climbing on it, asked. "Can I make the cake?"

"You can help me frost it, but that's later," Mama said as she mixed the cake batter. "Go play outside."

"Okay," Ann said, climbing off of the chair. She scurried out of the house and joined Lou in the pasture.

"What are you playing?" Ann asked.

"I'm playing tag," Lou said.

Ann frowned. "With who?"

"Missy and Rex, of course," Lou said. Rex was Grandmother's dog.

"How can *they* play?" Ann asked.

Lou scoffed, "You tag them and then run away. Then they start chasing you and once they catch you, you're it again."

She demonstrated by tagging Missy and sprinting away. Missy bolted after her. She quickly caught up to Lou and jumped up, "tagging" Lou's arm with her paw. Lou squealed, "See?"

Ann thought for a moment. "Can I play?"

"Sure," Lou said.

Ann and Lou played with Missy and Rex until it started raining. The runoff collected to form puddles of mud in the open pasture. Missy and Rex rolled in the mud and tried to jump on Ann with their muddy paws.

Mama sent Chrissa to bring both girls back inside before they ruined their dresses. Chrissa and Ann ran to the house while Lou trudged along behind them.

"Mama!" Chrissa squealed when they reached the porch. "Jack is eating mud!"

"It's all over his hands and shirt," Ann said, wrinkling her nose.

Mama gasped and flew onto the front porch.

"Where did he get mud?" she asked as she tried to get it out of his reach.

"Dunno," Chrissa said, shrugging.

"Uh, is something burning?" Mae asked, walking to the front door.

"The cake!" Grandmother Bates exclaimed, throwing herself out of her chair and into the kitchen.

Mama put Jack, who was still dirty, on her hip. "Wait, is that Lou?" she asked, squinting at the pasture.

Sure enough, Lou was playing in the muddy pasture with Missy and Rex again. Mama had a fit when she realized this. Much scolding followed Lou inside the house, where the only thing keeping Loretta from laughing was the stern look Grandmother cast in her direction.

After Lou changed into one of Meme's old dresses, the Moore girls went outside to sit on the covered porch and wait for their cousins to arrive. Water trickled over the roof into little puddles below.

"Lou, you mustn't stick your feet out into the rain like that," Mae chided. "You'll get wet again."

"Mama's already angry with you," Chrissa said.

Lou lifted her chin. "I'm not doing anything wrong. Mama never said I couldn't get my *feet* wet."

"It's not ladylike to greet your guests without shoes," Mae said.

"They're not my guests, they're Grandmother's," Lou retorted.

Mae argued, "They *are* your guests. They're family."

"What's that sound?" Ann asked.

"It's only the rain," Lou said.

Ann insisted. "No. I heard something."

"Look!" Chrissa said, pointing down the dirt road.

Sure enough, here came a wagon down the drive. Mama flung the door wide open and announced Aunt Mabel's arrival to Grandmother and Grandfather.

The wagon stopped in Grandmother's yard. Out popped four kids who ran to take shelter underneath the porch. Aunt Mabel and Uncle Jimmy followed, greeting the adults who had gathered on the porch.

Mama and Aunt Mabel embraced each other for a long moment. The kids around them chattered and became acquainted with one another while Grandmother Bates watched her daughters with love.

Mama pulled away from Aunt Mabel and studied her. "It's been a long time."

"It really has," Aunt Mabel said.

Mama noticed the kids' chatter and laughed. "I was going to introduce you all, but I see you have already met. Girls, these are your cousins. Anthony is eight, Thomas is five, Rose is two, and Noah is almost one." Mama said, pointing to each. "And these are my girls. Mae is nine, Lou is seven, Chrissa is four, and Ann turned three today."

The kids waved at each other.

Aunt Mabel squinted down the long driveway. "Here comes Amy."

A second wagon pulled into Grandmother's yard and out climbed a young woman with a small baby. A young man, who's laugh echoed around the pasture, escorted them to the porch.

The woman, Aunt Amy, passed her baby to her husband before tackling Mama in a ferocious hug. The two women wiped away tears and laughed with happiness.

"I've missed you so very much," Aunt Amy said.

"I don't think you've missed me more than I've missed you," Mama said.

Grandmother put an arm around each daughter. "Well, I've missed the both of you. See? This is why you should stay in Newark."

Mama and Aunt Amy laughed.

The cousins, aunts, and uncles were guided into the house after they tried to stomp the mud off of their shoes. The cousins played with their dolls and rubber band guns in the living room while the adults gathered in the kitchen, talking about past memories and laughing together.

SIX

THUNDERSTORMS AND MALARIA

APRIL 1935

It was the spring of 1935, and the flowers were just peeking their heads out from underneath the snow. The vegetables in Mama's garden were glad to glimpse the sun again, and the little furry animals were making their first appearances since last November.

Mama and her children were still living on Boss Allen's property. Mama sharecropped with Grandmother and Grandfather Bates during the week. On the weekends, when the girls didn't have school, they would help Mama harvest the cotton fields.

Jack was now one-year-old, full of curiosity and mischief. Ann was about to be four, and her favorite thing to do was babble away about random and often strange subjects. Chrissa was still very prim and loved to be dolled up by her aunt, Loretta. Eight-year-old Lou didn't like Loretta much. Loretta pranked Lou far too often to earn her respect. Mae was still Mama's helper who enjoyed telling Lou, and sometimes Loretta, what to do.

One evening while Chrissa and Ann were playing with their dolls in the front yard, it began sprinkling. Chrissa jumped up and ran inside to take shelter, shrieking about the rain. Ann continued to play in the yard until Mama called her inside.

One hour later the rain intensified. Thunder echoed along the valley, and lightning lit the ebony sky for only a fraction of a moment. Chrissa and Ann tried to act brave, but after a few minutes of the thunder's low growling, they took to hiding underneath the quilt Mama was working on.

Soon the sound of wagon wheels rumbling along the muddy driveway alerted Missy, who alerted the rest of the family. Mae jumped up and opened the front door to see Grandfather Bates hobbling out of his wagon.

He hurried into the house and stood, dripping, in the doorway. "Amerie, you have to come with me back to the house." He spoke too loudly inside the house. Ann covered her ears with her hands, causing Chrissa to giggle.

"Why?" Mama asked, setting down her quilt.

"The White and Black Rivers flood when it rains. This house is mighty close to the White River."

"Boss Allen wouldn't let us live in this house if it was unsafe," Mama chided, picking her quilting back up.

"Boss Allen lets people live here, even though it *is* unsafe. It's one of the prices of sharecropping." Grandfather sounded bitter.

"Your house isn't any further from the White River."

"Our house is near the top of a hill."

"This house is also at the top of a hill."

"This house has flooded before, and it can flood again."

Mama sighed and thought for a moment. "The kids have school tomorrow, and the bus only stops near our house."

"So, you won't come with me?" Grandfather asked.

"No," Mama said. "The kids have to get to school tomorrow."

"At least promise that you will keep an eye on the river. If the river reaches your porch, there will be no turning back. It will have surrounded your house. You have to watch," he said as a final warning.

"I will."

Grandfather tipped his hat at the girls before hobbling back to his wagon and drenched horses.

Mama chuckled to herself, resuming her quilting. "That was relatively easy. If Grandmother had come to get us, she would have insisted that we come with her and wouldn't have left until we did."

"Why are you hiding underneath Mama's quilt, Chrissa?" Lou taunted. "You scared?"

"Yes," was the mumbled reply.

"Me too," Ann said, poking her head out from underneath the quilt.

Lou picked up the sock she was supposed to be knitting. "I'm not scared of it."

A low rumble started in the distance, gradually working its way up to a roar above the house. The hanging oil lamps shook, and some were extinguished by the jostling walls. Chrissa and Ann shrieked again, taking shelter underneath the quilt.

Lou glanced at the walls. "I'm not scared," she said again, this time without confidence.

"Oh come off of it, Lou. You're scared of thunder," Mae said, watching the shawl she was knitting.

"Am not," Lou said, scrunching up her nose.

"Are too," Mae said.

A look from Mama stopped their bickering.

The rest of the night was passed in peace. As much peace as the thunderstorm would allow. Chrissa and Ann screamed at every rumble, and Jack thought it was a game. He started screaming with them, and they were all told to hush for the rest of the evening.

Mama worked on her quilting while Mae and Lou knitted until it was time for bed. Chrissa and Ann crawled into their trundle bed, whimpering at every roll of thunder until they were asleep. Mae and Lou slept soundly, and Jack didn't notice the thunderstorm at all. Mama, however, stayed awake most of the night, repeatedly stirring to check the river's height.

Early in the morning, Mama woke from a fitful sleep to check on the river again. The thunderstorm had stopped, and now the clear sky sparkled with twinkling stars and a full moon. The wind whistled through the leaves, and another sound came from outside. Mama couldn't quite determine what was making the sloshing sound.

She opened the back door and muffled a scream with her hand. The water was lapping at the back porch, glinting in the light of the full moon. It had risen rapidly while she slept, and now there was no way to leave the house. They had no wagon, no horses, and no way to escape the water surrounding the house.

Mae and Ann stumbled to the door, rubbing their eyes.

"What's the matter, Mama?" Mae asked.

"The river," Mama said, her hand still covering her mouth.

Mae's eyes got wide. "How did the river get all the way up here?"

"It rose during the night," Mama said, dropping her hand. She didn't take her eyes off of the river.

"But it stopped raining, so it can't come any further," Mae said.

"It might rise if it rains upstream," Mama said. Then, noticing the horror on Mae's face, she said, "Come inside, girls. Let's go back to bed."

Though Mama watched the river for the remainder of the night, the water never reached the top of the porch. The girls awoke early to check on the river and rejoiced to find that there would be no school that day. They begged Mama to allow them to wade in the newly formed lake in their backyard, and Mama consented.

The girls hiked up their skirts and tiptoed in the knee-deep water, giggling and splashing each other. After a few minutes, they could hear the faint paddling of Grandfather's fishing boat coming towards the house.

"Mama! Grandfather Bates is here!" Lou shouted into the house.

Mama walked outside with Jack on her hip and laughed as Grandfather waved his hat enthusiastically.

"How y'all doin' this morning?" he yelled.

"Mighty fine. And you?" Mama replied, laughing again.

"I'm just pretty as a peach. Look at what I caught you, here,"

Grandfather said, raising a tin pail for the girls to see. Long catfish swam inside of it, tapping the metal edges and trying to find a way to escape. He accidentally tipped the pail too far, and one of the catfish fell out.

"Well dang," Grandfather said, but not those words exactly.

Weeks later, the water was still there in stinky, gross puddles. It was stagnant and had grown mosquito larvae. There were so many mosquitos that Mama could not open the door without letting a few in. She no longer allowed the girls to play in the water, to their disappointment.

The school bus could not reach them because sections of the road were ruined by the flood. Mama tried to teach the girls reading and writing while at home, but she eventually gave up on that.

Mae was seated on a chair one afternoon, working on her shawl, but looking mighty pale. She continued to put her work down and stare blankly at the wall until some loud noise from Ann or Jack would bring her back to the present. She would pick the knitting up again, just to repeat the whole cycle a minute later.

After a few moments, Mama noticed what was happening. "Mae, are you okay?"

Mae sighed, "My head hurts."

"Maybe you should go lie down on the bed."

Mae nodded. She struggled to her feet and walked in a daze to the bed. Mae laid down and fell asleep, not to wake up for a long while.

Hours later, Mama checked Mae's temperature with her hand. Her forehead was burning hot, and she kept shaking with chills. Mama looked worried for the rest of the afternoon, and Ann noticed that she would cast glances at Mae every couple of minutes.

"What is wrong with Mae?" Ann asked as she toyed with Cobweb Windowlight's dress.

"She must have Malaria," Mama said.

"What is Malaria?" Chrissa asked, sitting on the floor beside Ann.

"Malaria is a sickness that is carried by mosquitoes," Mama said, glancing out the window. "It makes people sick, and you have to take a bitter medicine to feel better."

"Are you going to give Mae that medicine?" Ann asked.

"When I go to town tomorrow, I will get some medicine for her," Mama assured Ann.

The next day, the five children were left at home while Mama went to town for medicine. By the time she got back, Ann was not feeling well.

Mama sighed, "Oh dear." She picked up Ann and set her in bed beside Mae. Mae didn't stir as Ann snuggled close and fell asleep.

"Mama, these mosquito bites hurt," Lou said, scratching her arm furiously.

"Quit scratching or they'll feel worse," Mama chided.

By evening time, Chrissa had also been laid in the bed. The next morning, Jack was sick. Finally, Lou admitted to feeling sick and joined the other kids in bed. They were all sick with Malaria.

Mama gave each child quinine to feel better, but she had to mix it into hot chocolate so that they would take it. Even with the hot chocolate, the bitter taste seeped through, and the kids were reluctant to drink it.

Mama checked everyone's temperatures regularly, but Mae's temperature worried her the most. One night, Mae started talking and groaning to the wall. Mama rushed to Mae's side with a cool cloth for her forehead.

"Mama, what is happening to Mae?" Chrissa asked uneasily.

"She is really sick," Mama answered.

"Who is she talking to?" Ann asked.

"No one, sweetie."

"Look at me, Mae," Ann whispered, trying to turn Mae's head to face her.

Mama said, "She's not talking to anyone, Ann. She's talking out of her head."

"Talking outta her head?" Lou asked.

"She doesn't realize what she is saying," Mama explained.

"How?" Ann asked.

"Why?" Chrissa said.

"That's enough questions for right now," Mama said, returning to her bowl of cool water.

For a few days, it was the same routine. Mama sat up all day and all night, caring for her sick children. Then each one gradually gained their strength back. They were able to play quietly on the floor with their toys.

Mae was the last to get better. After a bit, she gained her strength back. Soon she was running and playing with her younger siblings, with a sigh of relief from Mama.

SEVEN
WILDCAT HOLLOW AND THE BENNETTS
JUNE 1936

CHRISSA CRIED, "DON'T PUSH, Lou!"

"'Betcha I'll be the first to see the whole house," Lou shouted as she jumped out of the wagon and raced up the porch steps.

"Wait for me!" five-year-old Ann hollered.

"Don't run in the house," Mama said as Ann raced past her.

Uncle Prichard laughed, "They're just excited to move, Amerie."

"They could stand to be a little less excited, or it'll be *my* nice china dishes that get broken."

Uncle Prichard laughed again as he hefted the box of Mama's china dishes out of his wagon and onto his shoulder. Mama took two-year-old Jack out of the wagon and let him chase his older sisters into the house.

Uncle Prichard walked in with the box of dishes, which he placed on the kitchen floor. After catching the attention of the girls, he led them to the wagon where he handed them items to bring inside. When the wagon was fully unloaded, Uncle Prichard blew kisses to the girls and drove back to his house.

The house was a nice log cabin with two rooms: one big kitchen and living room and one tiny bedroom. Two doors on opposite sides of the house led to separate porches. The front porch was the largest, but the back porch was still big enough to hold Mama's wash tub and clotheslines for washing day.

There was an old, untilled garden at the top of a small incline. It was overgrown with weeds, but Mama knew exactly how she would use it during the coming year. The hay barn was across a seasonal creek from the house. The creek had no water in it, but moss and mushrooms grew on the nearby rocks and trees year-round.

Mama's bed was placed in the tiny bedroom to the side of the house. The girls' pallet was placed in the living room during the night and rolled up in the morning. Daddy's flag was hung near the back door where it could be seen from all areas of the house.

Mama sighed as she plopped onto the rocker, letting the kids explore outside. So many things had happened to get them to this strange community named Wildcat Hollow.

Soon after the girls overcame their case of malaria, they obtained another disease from the mosquitos, who were breeding in the stagnant water. The girls were sick for the entire summer and the beginning of autumn.

When Uncle Prichard heard about this, he insisted that Mama and the kids leave Boss Allen's property. Uncle Prichard offered Mama the one hundred and sixty acres he had homesteaded in the Ozark Mountains. There was a two-room house on the property, and a seasonal creek ran nearby. He said she could have it for one hundred dollars, so she readily agreed.

There was one problem with the deal, however. Uncle Prichard already had a tenant on the property. Mama and the kids had to wait for the tenant to leave, which would be another year. Uncle Prichard wanted them away from the mosquitos soon, so they moved with him for the year.

And here she was now, one year later, with a household to unpack and supper to cook. She exhaled as she stood up, grabbed her tin pails, and walked outside. Ann and Jack were playing in the dried creek bed.

"Do you know where Mae and Lou are?" Mama asked.

"No," Ann said, brushing her fingers along the mossy rocks.

"Well then, *I'll* go to the spring to fetch some water," she said. "Chrissa is inside the house. Keep an eye on Jack while I'm gone, and don't let him wander away."

Ann nodded as Mama walked into the woods.

Jack was busy building a rock tower. It kept tumbling over because he stacked too many rocks, but he persisted nonetheless. Ann hopped on rocks along the creek bed and picked moss off of the tree trunks to feed to some pretend animals. Lou and Mae joined them in the creek bed for a moment before exploring the barn.

Ann heard the low rumble of wagon wheels and looked up to see a wagon coming up the road. "Look, Jack. A wagon."

Jack peered down the road for a second before returning to his rock tower.

Ann kept feeding her pretend animals the moss from the trees and rocks. She didn't care that a stranger had come to visit.

The man driving the wagon walked up the front porch, not noticing Jack and Ann playing in the creek bed. After a minute, Chrissa slipped out of the back door and fled to the creek.

"There's a man here and he keeps knocking on the door," Chrissa gasped.

"He's probably looking for Mama," Ann said.

"But Mama's not here."

Ann shrugged.

"I wish Missy was here," Chrissa said.

"Me too," Ann said

"She would protect us."

"Why'd we have to leave her with Grandmother and Grandfather Bates?"

"Because she was getting too old for Mama to take care of," Chrissa said.

Ann sighed.

"The man left the porch," Chrissa hissed, clutching Ann's arm.

The man looked around the house and noticed the kids playing. He walked up to them and took his hat off.

"Excuse me, but where is your Mama?" he asked kindly.

"She's fetching water from the spring," Ann said, pointing into the woods.

"Thank you," the man said before walking in the direction Ann pointed.

Ann and Jack continued to play in the creek while Chrissa went back inside to play with her doll. Half an hour later, Mama and the man emerged from the woods, talking until they reached the front porch. The man set the pails of water on the porch and left with a promise to visit again.

This was not the last time they would see the man, who's name was Mr. Bennett. He did visit again, asking Mama to take a walk along the creek bed to his house. Mama agreed, and when she came back she was bubbling with excitement. They had planned to have supper the following Saturday so that their children could meet each other.

By the time Saturday rolled around, the girls thought they knew the Bennett children personally because Mama would not stop talking about them.

"Little Bessie is younger than you, Ann, and she just turned five a couple of days ago. Mr. Bennett is bringing a cake for us to celebrate her birthday this evening, isn't that nice?" Mama told Ann as they set the table. "And, Lou, you must promise not to play any pranks on Neena or Belle; they don't like that sort of thing, you hear me?"

The sound of a wagon stopped Mama's speech, and the girls flew outside to meet the guests. Four girls almost equal to the age and height of the Moore girls tumbled out of the halted wagon. Mr. Bennett and his older son climbed out and greeted the family.

Mama came outside to make the introductions. "Girls, this is Oswald. He's fourteen. This is Ruby, this is Belle, this is Neena, and this little one is Bessie. They are each a little younger than you," Mama indicated each one with a wave of her hand.

Oswald looked far too old to be fourteen, Ann thought. His brown eyes and curly brown hair aged his appearance tremendously. Not to mention he was tall. Very tall.

Ruby was slightly taller than Meme, with light green eyes and blonde braids that reached to the middle of her back. She smiled at Ann, and Ann immediately knew she would like Ruby.

Belle had gray eyes, and a tiny mole on her left cheek that was the pit a dimple when she smiled, which was often. A slight breeze blew her light brown hair in front of her face, and she brushed it back with a giggle.

Neena cocked her head slightly, sizing up the Moore girls with her deep brown eyes. She was shorter than Chrissa and didn't look much older than Ann. What she lacked in size and age, however, she made up for in personality.

Bessie giggled when her name was said, her brown eyes sparkling as her long blonde hair tumbled down her back. It had been pulled into a ponytail with a ribbon but had fallen already. Instead, she wore the ribbon on her wrist with the bow facing up.

"And these," Mama said, turning to the Bennett children, "are my girls. Clementine is the oldest, but we call her Mae. Next is Louella, who we call Lou. Then Chrissa, and then Mollyann, who we call Ann. The little boy running around over there is Jack."

The girls waved shyly at each other.

Mr. Bennett noticed their stiffness and laughed heartily. "Okay, girls, you may go play. We will call you when supper is ready. Oswald, grab the cake from the wagon and follow me inside."

Ann hadn't noticed it before, but Oswald walked with a limp, favoring his right leg. She watched him curiously as he hobbled to the wagon and took the cake off of the seat. When he turned around, holding the cake close to his chest, they locked eyes. His dark brown eyes were filled with a mixture of sadness and embarrassment, and he quickly looked towards the ground. Mama tugged Ann's arm discreetly, giving her a look that said, "don't stare," before leading Oswald and Mr. Bennett into the house.

The eight girls looked at each other for a minute longer. Neena started laughing, and then Lou, and soon all of the girls joined in.

"Do you want to play in the creek?" Mae asked when the laughter stopped.

"Sure!" five-year-old Neena said, and immediately took off, her brown hair blowing in the wind behind her. The rest of the girls ran after her, giggling and shouting.

"There's no water in it," Ruby said, stopping short at the edge and peering in.

"It's a seasonal creek," Lou said.

"It only has water in the spring," Mae explained.

"I found some water," Bessie said, pointing to a stagnant pool no larger than her tiny foot.

"Yuck," Chrissa scrunched up her nose.

"C'mon, Chrissa, come play in the creek with us," Mae said.

"No way," she said, perching on top of a rock at the edge of the bank.

"What do you play in the creek?" ten-year-old Ruby asked, tugging on one of her blonde braids.

"We pretend to feed our zoo animals," Ann said.

"Zoo animals?" Belle asked.

"Yeah. You feed them the moss that grows on the trees," Lou said, picking off some moss and shoving it in Belle's face.

Belle gasped and backed away, looking disgusted.

"I have a cheetah," Mae said, pretending to pet her cheetah.

"I want a ... snake," Lou said after some hesitation.

Chrissa shrieked.

"I'll have a horse," Ruby said, picking off some moss.

"Anyone can have a horse. It has to be a *fun* animal," Lou chided.

"Anyone can have a snake, Lou, just walk to the barn and you'll find one," Mae said with a grin.

Chrissa yelped, "I'm leaving," and took off towards the house.

"I want a horse when I grow up," Ruby said.

Belle interrupted, "Spider!"

All of the girls raced out of the creek in mock concern and collapsed onto the front porch, laughing.

"Supper's ready, girls," Mama said, carrying some bowls of soup. The soup was Mama's recipe, with ham and plenty of the vegetables she grew in her garden.

The girls sat on the edge of the porch, their feet dangling off the side as they ate and talked.

Lou scrunched up her nose, looking at the soup. "Don't like it," she muttered to herself.

"What?" Belle asked.

"I said I don't like this soup," Lou said just a little louder.

"Why not?"

"Too many vegetables," Lou said.

"If you don't eat it, you don't get cake," Mae said.

Lou grumbled a response and began eating in tiny bites.

Oswald and little Jack returned from the creek bed.

"Jack wanted to show me his stack of rocks," Oswald explained as he limped up the stairs and into the house.

"Why does Oswald walk funny?" Ann asked when the boys had gone inside.

Mae almost choked on her soup.

"Ann," Lou scolded, wide-eyed.

"You can't say things like that, Ann," Mae said.

"Yeah. You can think them, but you can't say them," Lou said, earning her a jab in the ribs by Mae.

"What? I was only joking," Lou promised.

"He had Polio when he was a baby," Neena said.

"What is Polio?" Chrissa asked.

"It's a disease that makes you paralyzed," Belle explained.

"But he's not paralyzed," Mae said.

Neena shook her head, "Not *fully* paralyzed. He can't move his left ankle."

"And his left leg has always been weaker than his right leg," Bessie mourned.

Ruby ducked her head and said in a low voice, "He had it lucky. I've heard some people die because of Polio."

Ann shuddered.

"You ever done hand songs before?" Neena asked, changing the subject.

"You mean a clapping game?" Lou asked.

"Sure," Neena said.

"I have," Ann said.

The other girls agreed. They each paired up and sang *Say, Say Oh Playmate* while clapping to the rhythm.

Say, say oh playmate,
come out and play with me,
and bring your dollies three,
climb up my apple tree.

Slide down my rain barrel,
into my cellar door,
and we'll be jolly friends,
forever more - more - more!

Oswald and Jack came back outside after a couple of minutes.

"Is it cake time?" Ann asked excitedly.

Oswald shook his head. "They kicked us out of the house."

Ann sighed as she stomped off the porch.

Some of the girls continued clapping games while others went out to play in the yard. At last Mama and Mr. Bennett called them in for cake. They whooped and shouted for joy. After singing happy birthday to Bessie, they each got a slice of the delicious cake.

Afterward, Mama and Mr. Bennett gathered them on the front porch.

"Kids, have you had fun this evening?" Mr. Bennett asked.

"Yes," they said.

"Do you like playing with each other?"

"Yes."

"Well," he glanced at Mama, who was beaming, "how would you all like to be brothers and sisters?"

There was a moment of shocked silence.

"Wait, you mean -" Oswald began.

"You're getting married?" Mae exclaimed.

"Yes," Mama said.

"You what?" Neena was shocked.

"Yes, well, you see -" Mr. Bennet began.

"We're gonna be sisters?" Ann said.

"You're getting married?" Ruby repeated.

"And we're gonna live together?" Belle said.

"In one house?" Lou said, appalled.

"Yes," Mr. Bennett said.

"And always play together and live together?" Bessie asked, climbing into Mama's lap.

"Yes, sweetheart. Live together and play together," Mama said, stroking her blonde hair.

"In one house?" Lou repeated.

"Whose house are we living in?" Oswald asked.

"This house. It's the biggest," Mr. Bennett said.

"Mr. Bennett, when will you and Mama get married?" Chrissa asked.

"Soon. Very soon. And please, don't call me Mr. Bennett. Call me Dad. Everyone else does," he chuckled.

EIGHT

THE MARRIAGE AND MOVING IN

AUGUST 1936

THE WEDDING HAPPENED within two weeks of its announcement. In the week leading up to the wedding, there was a scramble to get all of the furniture moved into the Moore's house before their extended family arrived.

Grammy and Pop, Dad's parents, were able to attend, along with Grandmother and Grandfather Bates, Aunt Mabel's family, and Uncle Roy's family. Dad's oldest daughter, Ellie, was visiting for the wedding along with her husband, Jack. Dad's oldest son, Hudson, was away at CCC Camp. In CCC Camp, Hudson built roads and trails for the National Parks.

"Why can't we sleep in the hayloft?" Lou grumbled, sliding further underneath the blanket she and Belle shared.

"The boys are sleeping in there," Ruby said.

"Yeah, and they have to sleep with the snakes," Ann said, her eyes wide.

"I would sleep on the barn floor," Lou said.

"Let's just hope the snakes don't crawl into our blankets tonight," Mae shuddered as she glanced around the porch.

Bessie started crying.

"It's okay, Bessie. I wasn't being serious," Mae said.

Chrissa huffed, "I wish I could sleep inside."

"It's not too bad out here," Belle said.

Ann knew she was lying.

"Go to sleep, girls," Mama said, opening the front door to peek her head out.

"Okay," the girls said.

Mama shut the door, and they continued their whispering.

"It's so humid out here," Neena said, throwing back her blanket.

Chrissa seized the blanket. "Hey! I want that blanket."

"Why couldn't we sleep at Dad's house with Grammy, Pop, Dad, and Ellie?" Bessie asked.

"Because there's barely any room for *them* to sleep, let alone eight girls," Ruby said.

Mae huffed and sat up. "This is what we get for wanting to see what being sisters will feel like."

"*I* didn't want to do this," Lou grumbled. She rolled off of the blanket she was sharing with Belle, Mae, and Ruby.

"Lou, is that necessary?" Mae asked.

"Yes," Lou said, laying face down on the bare wooden porch.

"I'm serious, girls," Mama warned through the window. "Tomorrow is a busy day."

The girls stopped whispering after that.

The next morning was a marathon to get everyone dressed and fed before the wedding, which would happen at eleven. Grammy, Pop, and Dad came to the house early to help get ready.

Dad was dressed in his best suit, hair combed back, and a nice pair of shoes that hadn't seen the light of day in three years. When he arrived, the girls gawked at how nice he looked, for he never dressed *this* nice, not even for church!

"Dad! Wow!" Ann said.

"You like it?" Dad asked, spinning so she could see.

"You look so fancy," Chrissa said.

"Why, thank you." Dad bowed, making the girls giggle. "Now, go get dressed. If we're late to our own wedding, I'll never hear the end of it."

Aunt Ester went outside to wake the boys in the hayloft.

"Keep Rose and Noah away from the hairpins," Aunt Mabel warned as she scrambled some eggs in the kitchen.

"Don't step on my dress, Lou," Chrissa screeched.

"Get your dress off the floor, Chrissa," Lou said.

"Ann, hold still so I can braid your hair," Grandmother said.

Ann grimaced against the tight pull of her french braids.

Aunt Mabel called the kids for breakfast.

"Don't shove," Louis grumbled at Oswald.

Oswald raised his eyebrows, and Louis glanced away.

"Honey, do you know where my tie is?" Uncle Roy asked.

"It's in our bag, dear," Aunt Ester replied.

"Ah, I see." Uncle Roy said. "And, uh, do you happen to know where our bag is?" He indicated the piles of strewn clothes, lost ribbons, single shoes, and random toys that clouded the living room floor.

By ten thirty, all eight girls had their best dresses and shoes on. Their hair was neatly combed and braided, thanks to Grammy and Grandmother. Oswald and Jack Isam were wearing their matching shirts, which Oswald hated but Grandmother loved.

Uncle Roy's family and Aunt Mabel's family went ahead to the pasture while Grandmother and Grammy lined the ten kids up in the yard.

"Lou, your dress is unbuttoned at the top," Belle chided, moving to button it back up.

"Don't fix it!" Lou said.

"But it's supposed to be buttoned," Mae said.

"I don't like when it's buttoned. It makes me feel choked," Lou said, rubbing the back of her neck.

"Why is it so hot out here?" Ann complained.

"Jack! Get outta that dirt before I whoop you," Grandmother Bates shouted.

"Your hair is blowing in my face," Neena said to Ruby.

"I can't hold my flowers anymore," Bessie said.

Grandfather Bates whistled, stopping all the chatter. Everyone looked at the front door and gasped in awe.

Mama glided out of the house. She was dressed in her "Sunday Best," a white flowered dress, and carried a bouquet of Morning Glories, her favorite flower. Her hair had been curled and perfectly framed her face.

Dad stood in complete silence, jaw dropped, staring at Mama. She blushed and walked down the porch stairs to him.

"You ready?" She asked, taking his arm.

"For what?" he said, still staring.

"To get married, silly," she giggled.

Dad blinked, then grinned. "Of course."

Mama and Dad walked towards the marriage site, the pasture. The kids and grandparents followed a respectful distance behind them, chattering and making lots of noise.

Dad leaned over and whispered something to Mama. Mama's laughter echoed off the treetops and bounced into the pasture.

The wedding was wonderfully short and sweet. The little kids weren't interested in the vows, and Grandmother and Grammy could only do so much to keep them in their seats. Mama and Dad didn't care. They barely noticed when Bessie yelped because Lou pinched her or when Chrissa fell off her seat because a bee flew next to her.

The kids thought the reception was the most enjoyable part of the wedding. Grandmother Bates had baked a three-tiered cake the day before. This, along with Grammy's sweet tea, was a wonderful pair.

Grandfather whipped out his fiddle to play some tunes, to which the guests danced until their feet were aching sore. When Grandfather was tired of playing his fiddle, the kids went into the pasture to play tag.

When the adults finished talking, the decorations were taken down and everyone returned to the house. Over the next few days, all of their extended family left until it was only the Moore and Bennett families.

The kids begged Dad to make them a gunny sack swing on the big tree in the front yard. He agreed, and after it was set up, it was never still. Every morning, afternoon, and evening there were always at least two children fighting over it. Mama said it was more of a curse than a blessing, to which Dad just laughed.

Since there were so many living in the house now, two beds were set up in the living room, one in the kitchen, and one in a little, closet-like room at the back of the house. These beds were still pallets, which were folded and stored out of the way during the day. All eight girls slept in the living room, Oswald and Jack shared the kitchen pallet, and Mama and Dad slept in the little room.

With all the pallets in the house, there was no room for both dining tables and all twelve chairs to fit inside. Mama and Dad put them on the front porch, and when it was not meal time, the chairs were stacked against the house.

And so, their adventure as a family of twelve began.

NINE

DANIEL AND THE LION'S DEN

AUGUST 1936

THE KIDS WERE outside playing on a humid summer morning two weeks after the wedding. The sun had not peaked over the tall trees tops, but every child felt the effect of its rays. The humidity felt like a physical presence, bearing on the skin of the sweaty kids.

Lou and Belle were fighting over the gunny sack swing again, each one swearing the other had it last. Mae was ignoring their shouts as she read a book on the front porch. Bessie and Ann were prancing around, pretending to be horses, while Jack tried to copy them.

Ruby and Chrissa were hosting a pretend tea party with their dolls under the shade of the porch. Neena had climbed the big tree and began throwing acorns at Oswald, who in turn tried to throw sticks up at her. This ended when he hit Lou with a stick and was tackled.

Dad came out of the house with a picnic basket and blanket, which he carried to the barn and put in the wagon. On his way back inside, he told Oswald to hitch up Winter and Lacey. Winter and Lacey were Dad's horses, designated to pull the wagon.

"Where are you going, Dad?" Ruby asked, following him to the porch.

"To the creek," he answered as he walked inside.

Ruby sighed. "I love the creek. I wish I could go."

"We have a creek here," Mae said, indicating the dry creek bed to her left.

"But the creek he is talking about is wonderful. Oh, it is just an amazing creek. It's nice and sandy, without rocks that poke your feet," Ruby said.

"And it doesn't dry up in the summer," Belle said, giving the swing to Lou.

"I wish I were going with him, but he must be fishing," Ruby said.

Dad walked out of the house, carrying another basket.

"Can I come with you to fish?" Ruby asked.

"I'm not going to fish," Dad said. "We're going to swim. Get dressed and hop in the wagon."

Ruby gasped, and then began shouting, "We're going swimming! We're going swimming."

The kids ran inside, yelling and whooping for joy. Within just a few minutes, the entire family was ready to go to the creek. The wagon wheels creaked and groaned as it jostled along the dirt road. The girls chattered and squealed with delight as they walked beside the wagon.

"I can't wait to dip my feet in that cool water," Mae said.

"Yeah," Chrissa said. "I'm so hot."

"Guys, look at this," Neena said, stopping along the side of the road.

The girls stopped walking to see what Neena was pointing at. The wagon rumbled along, slowly gaining distance between them.

"I think it's a smushed frog," Lou said, bending down to get a better look at it.

"Ew!" Chrissa squealed.

"I think I can pick it up," Neena said. She flopped the squashed frog, which was nearly paper-thin, into the palm of her hand.

"Nasty!" Chrissa squawked, fleeing the scene to catch up with the wagon.

"It's so thin," Ruby said.

"Can I hold it, Neena?" Lou asked.

Neena handed it to her carefully.

"Where'd its guts go?" Belle asked, examining the frog in Lou's hand.

"They're on the road," Lou scoffed.

"Bleh," Belle said, scrunching up her nose as she peered at the dirt road.

Ann leaned her head out of the covered wagon and yelled, "Y'all better catch up, or we'll leave ya!"

"C'mon, let's catch the wagon," Mae beckoned.

"Okay. Here, Belle, catch," Lou said, tossing the dead frog at her.

It hit Belle's face, and she screamed. "Don't you ever do that again, Louella! I'll tell Mama!" She ran her hands over her face and shook them off with disgust.

Lou laughed and raced towards the wagon with Belle close on her heels.

When they reached the creek, another wagon was already sitting there. Giggles and splashes were heard from the creek.

"I wonder who's here?" Mama asked as she climbed out of the wagon.

"Is that - wait. I know those kids," Neena said, squinting into the creek.

"Who are they?" Lou asked.

"They're the Phillips," Neena said.

"Really?" Ruby asked, peering into the distance.

Mama handed each girl something to carry. "There's no way to be sure until we go down there."

The kids helped carry things to the edge of the creek. The older girls helped Mama set up dinner while the younger kids pulled off layers. They were splashing in the creek before Mama could tell them not to.

"The water is so cold!" Belle squealed.

"It feels so good." Ann splashed water above her head.

"Ann, don't splash people," Neena said, shying away from the stray water droplets.

Ann smirked, "You don't like being splashed?"

"It's cold," Neena said.

Ann splashed her. Neena yelped in surprise before turning around to splash Ann back. But instead of splashing Ann, Neena accidentally splashed one of the Phillips boys, who had come to see who was playing. He joined, and soon all three were giggling and sloshing in the chilly water.

Ruby announced that dinner was ready. The rest of the kids ran to the picnic basket to grab their dinner. Ann, Neena, and the boy stopped splashing each other.

"I'm Clarke," he said, sticking his hand out to Ann.

Ann shook it. "I'm Ann Moore."

"That's my family over there." Clarke pointed to the family that was still playing in the creek.

"Yeah, I know them," Neena said. "We see you at church sometimes."

Ruby called Ann and Neena from the picnic basket.

"We gotta go, but maybe we can play after we eat," Ann said.

The kids scarfed down their dinner and ran back to play in the creek. The Phillips kids made their way to where the Bennetts were playing. They introduced themselves to the newest Bennett family members, the Moores. Lillian was the oldest at ten years old, Clarke was six, Maggie was five, and Reuben was four.

After the introductions were finished, the kids asked what they should play together.

"Let's play tag in the water," Lillian suggested.

"I don't wanna," Reuben said.

"You don't wanna because you're too slow," Clarke said, ruffling Reuben's hair.

Reuben ducked and covered his head with his arms.

"Let's explore downstream," Lou suggested.

"No, I wanna explore up here. Look, I think that's a cave," Neena said, pointing at the cliff that lined one side of the creek upstream.

"That's no cave. It's just a rock," Oswald chided.

"Let's split up, then. Some go up to the cave and others go down-stream," Mae suggested.

The kids agreed and split up. Ruby, Neena, Lillian, Ann, Reuben, and Mae went upstream while Lou, Oswald, Belle, Bessie, Maggie, Clarke, and Chrissa explored downstream.

The sound of falling water was incredibly loud, echoing off the cliff and into the trees. Damp soil and the smell of fish wafted around the creek. Sunlight streamed through the leaves like little fairies, dancing on the mossy rocks below.

"Where was the cave?" Ruby asked after they had walked upstream for a while.

"Just up here," Neena assured her.

"Ouch!" Lillian yelped. "That rock was sharp."

There was a splash in the creek behind them. Ann turned around in time to see Reuben shoot out of the water, giggling. He splashed her, and she shrieked before splashing him.

"C'mon, Reuben and Ann, or we'll leave you," Mae said over her shoulder.

Giggling, Reuben and Ann hurried to join the rest of the group, trying not to slip on the rocks.

"Look! It's right up there," Neena exclaimed.

Sure enough, the 'rock' was a cave. It was nearly four feet off of the ground, spewing crystal-white water. The small waterfall was roaring as many gallons of water fell into the creek below.

When the kids reached it, they found that the cave was large enough to walk inside. It was also pitch black and echoed ferociously.

"Let's go inside," Neena said.

"Absolutely not," Mae said, putting her hand out to block Neena.

"Why not?" Neena asked.

"We're already too far away for Mama to see us. If she knew we walked inside a cave without her permission, we'd get in *so* much trouble."

Neena shrugged it off. "I'm climbing up there."

"No!" Mae cried, but Neena was already climbing up.

"Don't fall, Neena," Ann said.

"Yeah, don't slip," Reuben warned.

"I won't," Neena said.

Good thing Jack stayed with Mama, otherwise he'd get hurt trying to follow Neena, Ann thought.

Neena was halfway up the waterfall when Ruby picked up a rock and tossed it into the cave. There was a squeak as Neena turned to glare at Ruby.

"Who made that noise?" Reuben asked.

"Not me," Neena said, climbing up.

A bat flew out of the cave, right above Neena's head. She squealed and jumped back into the creek. The bat squeaked and flew around while the group screamed and sloshed through the creek to return to the picnic area.

The Mrs. Phillips and Mama were talking when the kids arrived. The other group was still downstream, so they kept the story to themselves. They didn't dare tell Mama about the bats for fear she'd make them leave.

The kids played at the creek for all of the afternoon, and it was close to supper when Mama and Dad made the kids dry off to leave.

"Did you like the creek?" Dad asked the kids.

"I did," Ruby said.

"Me too," Ann said.

"We should name the creek something," Mae said.

"Oh, I know! Name it 'Daniel and the Lion's Den'!" Neena exclaimed.

"Why would we name it that?" Lou asked.

"I found a cave on the side of the cliff," Neena said.

"I was with her," Bessie said.

"You didn't go in it, did you?" Mama asked.

"No," Neena said.

Ann chimed in, "A bat flew out of the hole when Ruby threw a rock in there."

Mama's eyebrows shot up.

"It didn't hit anyone," Ruby said quickly.

"Either way, the cave looked like the story from the Bible," Neena said.

"Then we'll name it 'Daniel and the Lion's Den'," Mama said.

TEN

SCHOOL AND RUN, SHEEP, RUN

SEPTEMBER 1936

"MAE, WHAT IS SCHOOL LIKE?" Ann asked, snuggling underneath her quilt.

"Oh, Ann, school is so much fun," Mae replied.

Lou protested, "It is *not* fun."

"It *is* fun," Ruby said.

"Yeah, you can talk to your friends," Neena said, sitting up in her pallet on the living room floor.

"I can't wait to see Emma at school tomorrow," Neena said.

"And Lillian will be there too," Ruby said.

Mae squealed, "I can't wait to meet some new people."

"Do we walk?" Ann asked.

"Yes." Lou crossed her arms and huffed.

"Oswald has to walk with us," Neena said.

"He always gets us in trouble," Belle complained.

"It is his last year, though. Next year he will stay and help Dad with the farm work," Ruby said.

"I know you're talking about me," Oswald said from his bed in the kitchen.

The girls snickered and continued their conversation in a whisper.

Neena giggled. "Remember last year, on the first day of school, he was goofing around and fell in the mud, ruining his new britches?"

"You're *still* talking about me."

The girls laughed.

"Remember when Greta got stuck in the tree last year, Lou?" Mae asked.

"And they had to get some men to grab ladders and help her down," Lou giggled.

"Who is Greta?" Ruby asked.

"She was our friend at our old school in Newark before we moved here," Mae said.

Neena laughed, "I tore my dress on the swing once, so I had to wear my apron backward for the rest of the day."

"Last year Mae would always come home from school with her braids all dirty, and Mama would get angry with her because she had been doing cartwheels in the dirt," Chrissa said.

"At least I didn't break my shoe buckle after I threw it at a boy, heh, Lou?" Mae said.

By now the girls were rolling on the floor with laughter.

"Time for bed, girls," Dad said as he came inside from the barn.

Ruby tried to stop laughing enough to explain what was funny, but she couldn't. Her attempt just made all the girls laugh harder.

Mama walked in and put her hands on her hips. "Enough is enough, girls. It's bedtime." She blew out the oil lamp. "Goodnight."

The girls tried to be obedient and go to sleep quickly, but a few giggles escaped each one before they drifted to sleep.

The next morning all eight girls were up and getting ready long before it was time. Each one took a turn in front of the mirror, fixing her hair with an audience of seven behind her.

After a hurried breakfast and a frantic search for one of the books Bessie and Ann shared, which was in their satchel the entire time, they were on their way to school. The one-room schoolhouse was over half a mile away, but the weather was nice and the girls were looking for opportunities to show off their outfits, so they didn't mind.

Once they reached the schoolhouse, the older kids found their friends and joined them. Ann and Bessie stood in the school yard before spotting Maggie in a tree. She was talking to another young girl who stood at the base of the tree.

"Who's that girl Maggie is talking with?" Ann asked as they walked over to join them.

"That's Merrylin. She's the preacher's daughter," Bessie said. "She's super nice."

"Hi, Ann and Bessie," Maggie said, jumping off the tree branch and greeting the sisters.

"Hi," they said.

"I'm Merrylin. Who are you?" Merrylin asked.

"I'm Ann," she said.

"Nice to meet you."

They talked for a minute before they were joined by two more girls, identical twins.

"Hi, I'm Ellen, and this is my sister Jeanette," one said.

The girls waved hello.

"Do you like jumping rope?" Jeanette asked, pulling out a clothesline.

The girls said yes and took turns holding the rope for the others to jump. They chanted *Down In The Valley* to the beat of the clothesline.

> *Down in the valley*
> *where the green grass grows,*
> *there sat Janey sweet as a rose.*
> *Along came Johnny*
> *and kissed her on the cheek.*
> *How many kisses*
> *did she get this week?*

1, 2, 3, 4, 5...

A couple of minutes later, the bell rang from inside the schoolhouse. The girls put away the clothesline. Each one hesitated for a moment, looking at the daunting schoolhouse with an uneasy feeling. Then they joined hands and walked inside the schoolhouse together.

A slim lady, who looked to be in her mid-thirties, smiled at them as they approached the front bench.

"Good morning, girls. I am Miss Longwood, the teacher here in Wildcat Hollow. Is this your first year?"

Ann looked at the other girls, who weren't speaking up, before nodding her head.

"That's great. You may sit here on this front bench. What are your names?"

They introduced themselves.

"Nice to meet you, Merrilyn, Bessie, Maggie, Jeanette, Ann, and Ellen. If you need any help today, I will be at my desk." She gestured to the large oak desk in the opposite corner of the schoolhouse.

That's a messy desk, Ann thought, noticing the scattered papers and pens.

By now the rest of the kids had settled in their seats. Miss Longwood got the attention of the class and began her welcome speech.

"Welcome, class. For those who don't know me, I am Miss Longwood. It is nice to see your faces again, along with some new faces. We will begin slowly this morning, so turn to page three in your reader, younger class."

Ann flipped open her reader while Miss Longwood gave instructions to the older class. Page three was easy sight words, so she read through them.

I'm glad Mama taught us how to read this summer.

Bessie leaned over and whispered, "Do you know what these letters mean?"

"C-A-T spells cat. See?" Ann said, pointing out the letters.

"Very good, Ann," Miss Longwood said. "I had no idea you already knew how to read."

Ann was startled at her praises. "Mama taught me over the summer."

"But not me because we didn't know each other," Bessie explained.

"Well, that is completely fine, Bessie. I will help you with your reading right after I get Ann an older level reader."

Ann's eyes grew wide with excitement.

All morning they worked on reading, geography, and history. At noon they were released for dinner. The seven Bennett and Moore children passed around the dinner Mama had packed and then dispersed.

Bessie and Ann joined Merrilyn and Maggie underneath the tree by the road..

"School is fun," Maggie said.

"Yeah. Lou said it wouldn't be fun, but it *is* fun," Ann said.

"Lou doesn't like school," Bessie said.

Ellen, or maybe Jeanette, skipped up to them with her sister behind her. "Well, *I* like school."

"My brother didn't want to come today," Merrilyn said.

"Who is your brother?" Ann asked.

"I have two. Oliver and Wilbur are my brothers. They're older than me," Merrilyn said.

The preacher has three kids, Ann thought with a nod.

"I don't have a brother. Just a sister," Jeanette, or maybe Ellen, said, placing her hand on her twin sister's shoulder.

"I have an older brother and a younger brother," Maggie said.

"Yeah, Clarke and Reuben," Ann said. "We know them from the creek."

"But Reuben is too little for school. He will come next year," Maggie said.

Neena ran to the girls. "We're gonna play Run, Sheep, Run. Do you wanna play with us?"

"What is Run, Sheep, Run?" Merrilyn asked.

"It is a game where you pick two teams and you hide and - oh just come on. They'll explain it when we get there," Neena said, grabbing Bessie's hand and running towards a large group of kids.

The other girls finished their dinner and hurried to join the gathered group of kids. The oldest boys, who were bossing everyone around, were inside the circle. It seemed to Ann that all the schoolchildren were here.

"Ralph and I will be the team captains. Get in a line and we'll choose our teams," Oswald was shouting.

"Why are you the team captains?" asked Oliver.

"Because we are the oldest," Ralph said.

"And because the team captains don't have to run," Oswald said, indicating his left leg.

Oliver's eyebrows shot up. He'd forgotten how much pain Oswald's limp caused him when he ran.

The group lined up facing Oswald and Ralph. The boys took turns picking people from the line to be on their team, starting with the oldest and fastest and then moving on to the "weaklings." Ann was one of the last to be put on a team, and it was Ralph's team.

"You are the sheep first since I picked first," Oswald said once the teams had been picked.

Ralph agreed and told his team to huddle up. "Does everybody know how to play this game?"

Ann and some other kids shook their heads "no."

"We're the sheep. That means we hide and try to get to the sheep pen, that tree over there, without being found by the foxes. No one moves unless I give the signal, you hear me? I'll show you where I want you to hide. I'll shout some signals, and you must know what they mean. Listen closely.

"Red means danger, so get away quickly if the foxes are near you. Blue means you're okay. Stay where you are because we aren't coming near you. Green means to move slowly towards the sheep pen, which is the tree near the road. All the other colors mean nothing, they are just to throw off the foxes. And when I yell 'run, sheep, run,' you must run as fast as you can to the sheep pen. Everyone got it?"

The new kids shook their heads "no" again.

Ralph sighed. "I'll pair a younger one with an older one. Clarke, you take Maggie."

"No way," Clarke said.

Ralph rolled his eyes. "Fine."

Clarke doesn't want Maggie because she's his sister, Ann thought.

Ralph gave all the younger kids an older pair. Ann's was Lillian Phillips. Ralph led the group around the schoolyard, finding places to hide. Ann and Lillian hid behind the broken shed.

When everyone was hidden, Ralph went to get the other team, the "foxes," and let them search for the sheep. They began walking towards Ann's left as a group. Ralph called out, "Clarke, red. Clarke, blue. Ellen, orange. Wilbur, green. Clarke, silver," and the like, throwing off the foxes. They began walking towards Ann, and she heard Ralph yell "Lillian, red."

"C'mon," Lillian whispered, crawling away. Ann followed as they crouched behind the bushes, trying not to make any noise.

Ralph yelled "Wilbur, pink. Lillian, blue," and then continued shouting random colors. Lillian popped her head up and looked. The foxes were walking in the opposite direction.

"We stay here until he calls red to us again or says 'run, sheep, run,'" Lillian whispered to Ann.

They sat in the bushes, watching the foxes walk in circles as Ralph shouted colors. Suddenly Ralph shouted, "Run, sheep, run!"

Immediately Lillian seized Ann's hand and sprinted through the bushes towards the tree, the safe zone. Foxes began racing back to the tree too. It was a scramble to see who's team would reach the tree first.

The last two foxes ran up as the final sheep touched the tree.

There was a tremendous shout of victory from Ralph's side and a chorus of "good game" from each team.

Miss Longwood called the kids in from their dinner break soon afterward. The rest of the afternoon was spent in grammar and arithmetic, but Ann's head was spinning from the excitement of the game for the rest of the day.

ELEVEN

THE BARN SWING AND RIDING AUSSIE

It was a clear, sunny day in May. The birds were chirping way up in the treetops and the water in the creek trickled over the mossy rocks. All the kids enjoyed the cool relief of the creek because they knew it would dry up soon.

It was Ann's sixth birthday, and she wanted the Phillips to join them for her birthday supper. Mama agreed, and the whole morning was spent in preparation for the guests.

After dinner, however, the kids had become restless inside the house. They were fighting, throwing things, and jumping on the pallets. Mama had enough of it and kicked them out of the house.

"I call the swing," Lou yelled as she walked out the front door.

"Not fair, Lou. You had the swing the whole time yesterday. It's my turn," Bessie said, running after her.

"I want a rocker," Chrissa said.

"Me too!" Ruby said. They raced out the door.

By now everyone was scrambling outside, fighting over places to sit and wait for the Phillips.

"I want to play in the barn, Mae," Ann said.

"Well then go play in the barn," Mae replied, collapsing on the porch.

"She can't go in the barn alone. Mama thinks she'll fall off the loft," Neena yelled, as she ran to the tree.

"I don't want to go in the barn right now," Mae said.

"Please?"

"No, Ann."

Ann stalked off to pout in a corner of the porch as Belle screamed.

Oswald began laughing as Belle wriggled and twisted until a small brown object fell out of her shirt.

"Don't you ever drop a June Bug down my shirt again, Oswald," she cried. "Or I'll tell Dad."

Oswald just kept laughing.

The usual scuff and chatter continued amongst the children as they waited for their long-expected guests. Ann complained to Mae about wanting to play in the barn. Chrissa and Ruby played with their dolls on the porch. Neena threw acorns off the tree, occasionally hitting Lou or Bessie.

"Is that a wagon coming down the road?" Mae asked, squinting.

"Of course not. It's just a shadow," Lou scoffed.

"No it's not," Ann said. "Look."

Sure enough, along rumbled a wagon down the road, kicking dust into the trees. Clarke and Reuben hung off of the edge of the wagon, waving and cheering as they pulled up and stopped in the driveway.

Mama walked out of the house and greeted Mrs. Phillips. Mae leaned over to Ruby and whispered something - Ann heard the word baby - while pointing to the two women.

"You don't know that," Ruby said.

"I heard them talk about it last month in the kitchen," Mae said.

"That's rude, Mae. What if it isn't a baby?" Ruby asked.

"Mama's having a baby?" Ann asked, a little too loudly.

Mae's eyes grew wide and she leaped to cover Ann's mouth with her hand. "Shhh," she hissed. "You can't walk around saying that, Ann. It's rude."

"But you said-"

"Hush," Mae interrupted as Lillian approached them.

Mama's belly has grown lately, Ann thought, studying her Mama, *but what if that's just because of all the birthday cakes? There are lots more birthdays now.*

Ann brushed her questions away when Maggie ran to her from the wagon.

"Let's go play in the barn," Lillian said. The kids agreed and raced across the creek to the barn.

Oh, now *Mae wants to play in the barn,* Ann frowned.

Now, the barn was a major attraction to all the children who visited the Bennett house. It was a favorite not because of the friendly cows or nice horses, for they were kept in the pasture until night, but because of the hayloft and barn swing.

The barn swing was attached right in the middle of the roof and hung down to about three feet off the floor. The hayloft was high on the back wall and, of course, filled with hay almost year-round. Right after harvest the hay would be so much that it spilled onto the floor below.

In the race to get to the barn, Clarke arrived first, followed soon by the older girls, a limping Oswald, and then a string of panting young ones.

Clarke climbed into the hayloft, took hold of the swing, and jumped as far as he could off the ledge. The swing caught him, and he sailed up the other barn wall. The kids crowded into the barn to watch him slowly come to a stop.

When the swing stopped, the other kids made a line below the ladder to the hayloft. Ann took her place behind Belle before anyone could steal it.

After Clarke came Oswald. After Oswald came Lillian, who squealed when she jumped from the loft but burst into laughter soon afterward. Neena swung off, proud that she didn't yell one bit, and Lou went upside-down right after her.

About this time Chrissa inched into the barn and stood near the door, as if ready to run out should some creeping bug or angry animal advance towards her.

"C'mon, Chrissa, get in line and do the swing," Clarke said, waving his hand to indicate the line.

Chrissa shook her head defiantly. "If I wanted to get my dress filthy and ruin my hair, I would go running around with the horses," she said, flattening her dress against the wind.

Ann shrugged and turned her attention to the swing, which Belle had just vacated. Ann scrambled up the ladder and caught hold of the swinging rope. She sat in the loop and, after a moment's hesitation, jumped off the edge. A rush of excitement coursed through her body as the swing sailed up the other side and back down again.

Before she knew it, her time was up. She reluctantly climbed off and tossed the swing to Bessie, who was waiting impatiently in the hayloft.

The kids spent the majority of the afternoon climbing into the hayloft and jumping onto the swing. Lillian, Ruby, and Mae eventually became bored of the swing and wandered off, Oswald at Lillian's heels. The rest of the kids were persistent and stayed at the barn until Mae called them for supper.

Supper was beans and cornbread, Ann's favorite meal. Cornbread was a rare treat. Mama baked a lovely vanilla cake with chocolate-flavored icing for Ann's birthday, which the children devoured in seconds. After supper, the kids went back outside to play until dusk when the Phillips would have to leave.

The children walked into the barn but were dismayed to find that Dad had already put up the cows and horses. They were not allowed to use the swing when the animals were inside, Dad said, lest they accidentally hurt one of the animals or themselves.

They were just turning away dejectedly when Clarke had a wonderful idea.

"What if I try to ride Aussie?" Clarke asked.

Aussie was Dad's milk cow; a mean, old lady cow who didn't enjoy children. Aussie's five calves had been a tremendous help to Dad on the farm, and he had recently decided to let Aussie enjoy a little "retirement." Although Aussie was supposedly living her last year on earth, she was as healthy as ever, and Dad joked that she might end up living longer than her five children.

"You can't ride Aussie. She's mean and will buck you off before you even get started," Oswald scoffed.

"I bet she'll let me ride her," Clarke said, swatting Aussie's rear. Aussie mooed and glared at Clarke.

Bessie giggled. "You can't ride Aussie. She's a cow, not a horse."

Clarke shrugged. "I think I'll be able to ride her."

"We have to ask Dad," Belle said, and Lou dashed to the house to ask.

Dad laughed after Lou told him the story. "If Carrie is alright with it, I'd be okay with him trying to ride Aussie. She won't let him, but he can try."

Lou turned expectantly to Mrs. Phillips, who glanced at Dad.

"Don't worry, Carrie. Aussie is a good cow. She won't hurt him. He might get a few scratches from falling off, but nothing worse than that."

Mrs. Phillips sighed. "I guess he can, but keep the younger children out of the way."

Lou squealed and was on her way out of the door when Dad shouted, "Make sure Oswald puts Aussie back up when they're done."

"Yes, sir," Lou shouted over her shoulder, racing out of the house where she began crying with glee, "He can, he can, he can!"

Oswald had gotten Aussie out of the barn by the time Lou ran up, panting. Clarke studied the cow, who was chewing her cud. She was much bigger up close.

"You gonna do it, Clarke, or are ya a coward?" little Reuben taunted.

Clarke crossed his arms. "I *am* gonna ride her. I'm no coward." He advanced toward Aussie.

Oswald dropped the lead rope and retreated to protect Lillian.

Clarke walked back a few steps, took a running start, and tried to leap onto Aussie's back. He bumped into her side and landed on the floor while the kids laughed. Aussie ignored it, still chewing.

He tried again. This time he landed with one leg over her back but slid off before he could grab her neck. The last time he tried, he was able to pull himself onto Aussie. She did not like this and reared, bucking him off. He landed in the grass with a thud as the children laughed.

Clarke tried two more times before giving up. Oswald put Aussie away as the kids snickered and dispersed to play their separate games.

It was just beginning to get dark when Mama, Dad, and Carrie walked out of the house and called the children from where they were playing in the pasture. The Phillips climbed into their buggy and drove away to the dismay of the Bennett and Moore children, who were told to dress for bed.

TWELVE

LOST TREASURE AND A PIRATE SHIP

APRIL 1938

IT WAS "the most humid day in the entire world," as Ann complained that morning.

"It's not that humid outside," Mama insisted.

It is that humid, Ann thought.

The smell of damp soil filled the air as the creek roared, having sprung to life from the recent rain. The cloudless sky allowed the sun's rays to filter to the ground through the leaves of the tall trees. The ground squished beneath them as the kids played dolls, shot rubber band guns, and climbed trees.

Mama and Dad had been married a year and a half, and each day brought another adventure. Mae had been right about Mama expecting a baby. On September 28, 1937, baby Wendell was born. Of course, it was a complete surprise to the younger kids, but nevertheless, everyone was excited to meet the newest member of the family.

On this humid day, Mae was still reading her book in the living room when Ann came inside. She grumbled, trying to get Mae's attention, but couldn't.

How can that book be more interesting than playing with me? Ann frowned.

Mama glanced at Ann from the kitchen where she was feeding six-month-old Wendell. "Ann, leave Mae alone. She's trying to read her book."

"But I want Mae to play with me," Ann complained.

"She's reading. Go play outside with your other siblings. You have ten."

Ann huffed. She didn't want to go back outside because she didn't want to play without Mae. She also didn't want to make Mama angry by disobeying. So she went outside.

Neena and Chrissa were in the middle of a heated conversation, each grasping the swing.

"Get your hands off the swing," Chrissa yelled. "I called it first, and you only beat me to it because you threw a bug at me."

"It was a moth," Neena said.

"I don't care. You get your hands off my swing, or I'll tell Mama."

"It's not *your* swing."

"Well ... I'll tell Mama," Chrissa shouted again.

"Is that a June bug beside your foot?" Neena asked, pointing. There really was a June bug, crawling along the ground and minding its own business.

Chrissa screamed and leaped away.

Though she tried not to, Neena laughed. Chrissa huffed and stomped into the house. She could not enjoy swinging when she knew a June bug was crawling right underneath her dress.

Ann collapsed on the grass. *If I look sad, maybe Mae will come out and play with me*, she thought while picking at the leaves. To her delight she only had to mope around for a couple of minutes before Mae came outside, bursting with excitement.

"I have the best idea," Mae announced after gathering some of the kids. "We should play pirates."

"Where?" Neena asked.

Mae thought for a minute, then pointed towards the barn. "The other side of the creek."

"Where's our ship?" Ann asked.

"All around the barn," Mae said.

"I want to be lookout," Neena said.

"Can I steer the ship?" Belle asked.

"I'm the captain!" Lou said.

"You can't be the captain," Ann retorted.

"I can too," Lou said.

"Mae thought of the game. She should be captain," Ann said, grabbing Mae's hand.

"Do you want to be captain, Mae?" Belle asked.

"Yes," Mae said, then noticed Lou's scowl. "But we can take turns."

Ann shouted, "Yay! Mae's captain."

Lou crossed her arms and stomped into the house, ignoring Mae's pleas for compromise.

"Just leave her," Neena said, waving her hand in the air.

She has to be angry before she can calm down, Ann thought.

"Ah! The floor is water," Bessie exclaimed.

"Everyone get on the ship, or you'll drown," Neena shouted.

There was a scramble to get across the creek and reach the safety of the "ship."

"What are we looking for?" Belle asked once everyone was gathered.

"Yeah, why are we playing pirates? Is there another pirate ship?" Neena said, shielding her eyes with her hand and looking around. "Do we have to defend our meek little ship from the invaders of the land?"

Mae thought about it for a minute. "I think we are looking for treasure. Yes, hidden treasure that our ancestors buried long ago."

"What is ancestors?" Ann asked.

"Ancestors are the people who were parents to our parents," Neena said.

"So, grandparents?" Ann asked.

"No, older than them," Belle said.

"Who can be older than grandparents?" Ann asked.

"Really old, dead people," Neena said.

Ann shuddered, "Oh."

"Let's look for hidden treasure with a map," Bessie said.

"What's the treasure?" Ann asked.

"The treasure is Mama's button box. But we have to sail our ship to the house before we can find it," Mae said.

"Where is the map?" Neena asked.

"In my head, of course," Mae said. "So set the course for the house, sailor Belle, and remember to keep the flag flying high."

And so their adventure for hidden treasure began.

The quest for the treasure lasted all of three glorious minutes before Oswald whistled from across the creek.

The kids stopped their game and looked in his direction. He was pulling Jack's red wagon with Lou, Ruby, Jack, and Chrissa inside of it. Lou stood in the wagon, balancing by holding onto Ruby and Chrissa's heads. Chrissa scowled and tried to remove Lou's hand.

"I have come with my pirate ship, and I'm gonna take over your ship, Mae," Lou shouted "Give up!"

Mae raised her eyebrows as Ann scoffed, "You can't take our ship. It's too big."

"And *your* ship is too small," Neena said.

"We won't let you take our ship," Belle shouted defiantly.

"'Course you won't *let* me," Lou said. "I'm gonna force it from you. If you let me take it it would be no fun."

"Well, you're gonna have to work hard to get this ship from us, Lou. We have the larger ground," Mae said.

"Well, we have the acorns," Lou said, and with that, picked up a handful of acorns and threw them across the creek.

The rest of her pirate crew caught the hint and picked up acorns of their own. Mae's group cowered behind trees but soon began finding ammo of their own to deal out to the attacking pirates.

Acorns flew across the creek, smacking everyone.

An acorn hit Bessie in the forehead and she immediately burst into tears. Jack threw his acorns harder after being hit multiple times. Mae had to take a break behind a tree when an acorn hit her in the eye. Lou was hit in the face so many times that she lost count.

Oswald had the best aim, but he was also the largest. Chrissa threw one acorn and then ran behind the house. Lou called her a coward.

After a couple of minutes, Mae called a halt to the acorn-throwing. She gathered her crew behind the barn and held a secret meeting, which Lou strained to hear but could not.

"What should we do? They aren't going to let us alone," Mae said.

"We should keep fighting until they get too hurt and go away," Ann said, scowling in their direction.

"Maybe we should give up the pirate ship and go find the treasure at the house," Belle suggested.

"No," Bessie said.

Mae's eyes lit up. "We should!" she exclaimed. "We'll pretend our ship was lost at sea, and we swam to the house, where we happened upon the hidden treasure we were searching for all along!"

The kids agreed and raced across the creek, splashing their confused opponents. And so, Mae's pirate crew was stranded at the house with their hands full of treasure, Mama's buttons. Lou's pirate crew had finally attained the ship they wanted and were searching the seas for more ships to capture.

And everyone was satisfied. At least, for the moment.

THIRTEEN

THE PAGEANT AND THE POTLUCK

DECEMBER 1938

CHRISTMAS BROUGHT good tidings and holiday decorations, something the kids loved. There was another fresh pine tree, decorated with popcorn strings and Mae's glass ornaments. Mama's nativity, which Daddy had carved for her during their first Christmas, sat on the mantle. It was a sad reminder to the Moore girls that Daddy couldn't share any more Christmases with them.

A fresh blanket of snow lay outside, untouched by the kids because Mama didn't want to clean them up after playing in it. There was to be a Christmas pageant that evening, and all the children in the church were to be in it.

The entire afternoon was dedicated to preparing for the church pageant. A potluck would follow the pageant, so Mama, Ruby, and Mae spent the afternoon baking Christmas goodies to share. The smell of fresh gingerbread, fruit cake, and chocolate chip cookies watered the mouths of every child stuck inside on that snowy afternoon. Twice Mama had to run Dad out of the kitchen because he took cookies when she wasn't looking.

Lou and Belle were put in charge of making the younger kids

rehearse *Away In A Manger*, which would be sung during the pageant. This was not going so well.

"Everybody hush so we can practice," Lou shouted over the chatter. The kids didn't stop talking.

"We have to practice before we can go play," Belle coaxed. "Let's all sit down and practice."

"We don't wanna," Ann complained.

"Mama said we have to," Lou said, folding her arms over her chest.

Jack looked at Mama, who took a basket and walked outside to collect the chicken eggs. He squinted and said, "Is Mama getting fat?"

Lou clapped her hand over her mouth as her eyes grew wide.

"Don't you *ever* say that about Mama again, Jack," Mae scolded in a hushed whisper.

Ann tried to hold back a snicker. *Mama has gotten pretty big, but that's just because she's expecting a new baby. At least, that's what Mae said.*

"What?" Jack asked, looking around innocently. "Her clothes don't fit no more."

"*Jack*," Ruby said, her mouth dropped open.

"Can we *please* focus?" Belle asked.

"Here comes Mama. Not another word, Jack," Mae warned as she turned back to the cookies in the oven.

A blast of chilly air followed Mama inside as the kids picked up where they left off.

"I don't remember the words to the song," Bessie said.

"I wanna go play," Neena said, looking wistfully out the window.

Lou groaned and collapsed onto the bed.

"Let's all sing through the song," Belle suggested. "If you forget the words, hum the tune. We can't go play until we practice, so everyone pay attention."

The kids reluctantly obeyed and sang through it half-heartedly. They rejoiced when Mama let them go play. The rest of the afternoon passed rapidly. All too quickly, Mama was packing food and children into the wagon.

They grabbed their heaviest coats, bundling up against the frigid weather. Dad heated some bricks in the fire and put them on the floor of the wagon. The children snuggled under blankets, and the heat from the bricks warmed their toes. The drive into town was a mile and a half, but before long, they reached the church.

It was a small church, only one hundred square feet. It had been the schoolhouse before the little town built a new, bigger one. The outside was painted white, but you could barely tell it because of the dust that stuck to the sides like glue. One cross stood on the roof; it had taken three men just to carry it up the ladder.

The inside was set up just as the schoolhouse had been. Four benches on each side lined up with the windows on the wall. The blackboard was still on the front wall; it had a different Bible verse written on it every Sunday morning. A clock hung above the door, to which every young pair of eyes would drift at some point during the sermon.

The church had sixteen seats available, but over thirty people attended every Sunday. They were in desperate need of a new building, but until the money could be found, nothing could be done about it. The church members took to stacking younger children on top of the older children and making everyone else sit on the floor. This partially solved their problem, but a few men still had to stand in the back every Sunday.

Now the church was even more crowded. The pageant had been moved inside because of the frigid weather instead of being held outside. Children were running around the benches playing tag, mothers were carrying dishes of yummy food, and fathers were talking near the rear of the church about the wheat crop.

None of the children had to dress up except for Mary and Joseph. Mary was played by Lillian. She wore a simple dress, had a scarf tied around her head, and carried her doll to play baby Jesus. Oswald was Joseph because he was the oldest boy and because Ralph Poher didn't want to pretend to be married to Lillian. Oswald had one of Dad's old coats on and carried a stick he found on the road.

Oliver, Clarke, Merrilyn, and Ann were shepherds. They were led by Ralph, who preferred playing a shepherd over Joseph.

The angels were Ruby, Ellen, Chrissa, Jeanette, and Bessie. Neena played the Angel Gabriel who told Mary of the coming of Jesus Christ.

Mae was the narrator who was supposed to keep all the kids on the right track, should they start goofing off.

Belle, Wilbur, and Maggie were the wise men. They were not particularly wise and most were not men, but they had been selected as those honored to play the part.

The youngest three kids were left as animals. Reuben was a cow, Jack was the donkey, and Wendell would be a sheep if she didn't cry during the pageant, Mama said.

Lou was the innkeeper.

After everyone arrived, the kids were taken to the back and instructed once more over the events of the story. Each one knew the story of the birth of Jesus Christ by heart; it was all old news to them.

"And remember, Ruby, to tell the angel choir to start singing *Away in a Manger* when you see the shepherds," Mama reminded her.

Ruby nodded her head.

"Just remember to have fun," Mrs. Phillips said.

"And stick to the general storyline," Mrs. Chinx added.

"We will sit down, and then, Mae, start the pageant," Miss Poher said.

Mae nodded as they walked to their seats and sat down.

Mae walked to the front of the church. "Welcome, ladies and gentlemen, to the performance of Jesus' birth." The crowd clapped, and Wendell squealed from the back. "I will be reading from the passage of Luke 2."

She opened Dad's Bible and began reading, "'And it came to pass in those days, that there went out a decree from Caesar Augustus, that all the world should be taxed. And this taxing was first made when Cyrenius was governor of Syria. And all went to be taxed, every one into his own city. And Joseph also went up from Galilee, out of the city of Nazareth, into Judaea, unto the city of David, which is called Bethlehem; (because he was of the house and lineage of David) to be taxed with Mary, his espoused wife, being great with child.'"

Mae closed the Bible. "We give you the story of the first Christmas."

Mae passed Lillian in the aisle as she walked to the back of the church. Lillian put her washbasin down at the front of the church and pretended to wash clothes. "My, what a lovely day," she said.

Neena ran to the front of the stage. "Hello, lady," she shouted.

Lillian almost fell over the washbasin. The kids in the back laughed but were hushed by Mae. "Who are you?" Lillian asked.

"I am the Angel Gabriel," Neena said, "and I've come to tell you that you are gonna have a baby."

"I am?" Lillian asked.

"Yes. And you will call him Jesus. Remember that name. J-E-S-U-S," she turned around and wrote it on the blackboard. "That's how you spell it."

The audience was laughing. Neena turned around and grinned when she realized they were laughing at her.

Lillian tried to keep a straight face. "When will he be here?"

"Nine months, obviously," Neena said, raising her eyebrows.

The audience continued to laugh, slapping their knees. The kids in the back were laughing again as Mae tried in vain to quiet them.

"Anyway," Neena said, "that's all I needed. Good day." And she ran off the stage.

Lillian looked around, confused, before following Neena to the back.

Mae walked to the front with the Bible. "'And so it was that, while they were there, the days were accomplished that she should be delivered. And she brought forth her firstborn son, and wrapped him in swaddling clothes, and laid him in a manger; because there was no room for them in the inn."

Mae closed the Bible and returned to the back. Lillian and Oswald walked to the front of the church, Lillian with a basket under her apron and Oswald leading Jack, the donkey, on a rope. Lillian gasped.

"I need a place to stay," she said.

Oswald dropped the lead rope and walked to an invisible door, behind which Lou was standing. He pretended to knock, stomping on the ground, and Lou pretended to open the door.

"Yeah?" she asked.

"We need a place to stay," Oswald said.

"Uh-huh" Lou said.

"Can we stay at your inn?" Oswald prompted.

"No," Lou said.

"Why not?"

"No room."

"What do you mean 'no room'?"

She cupped her hands around her mouth and shouted, "There's no room in the inn."

The crowd laughed again.

"Is there anywhere else we can stay?"

Lou thought for a moment. "No."

"Nowhere? Not even a barn?"

"No."

Oswald raised his eyebrows. "Stable?"

"No."

He rolled his eyes.

"Don't roll your eyes at me, young man," Lou said.

The audience was rolling with laughter.

"You're supposed to let me stay in the barn," Oswald whispered.

"It was a cave," Lou said.

"Does it matter? Show me the barn."

"Cave," she said defiantly.

"Fine," Oswald said, ending the whispered conversation. "What about a cave. Do you have a *cave?*"

"As a matter of fact, I do," Lou said. "Right over there where the cow is doing somersaults."

And she was not making it up, for Reuben had gotten bored of sitting on the floor mooing like a cow. He started showing off his tumbling skills. The audience laughed again, which prompted Reuben to do more flips.

Oswald guided Lillian and Jack, the donkey, to the cave.

Mae led the angels to the front. The younger ones gathered around the cave, hiding Lillian while she traded the basket for her doll. Mae read some more of the Bible story.

"'And there were in the same country shepherds abiding in the field, keeping watch over their flock by night. And, lo, the angel of the Lord came upon them, and the glory of the Lord shone round about them: and they were sore afraid. And the angel said unto them, Fear not: for, behold, I bring you good tidings of great joy, which shall be to all people. For unto you is born this day in the city of David a Savior, which is Christ the Lord. And this shall be a sign unto you; Ye shall find the babe wrapped in swaddling clothes, lying in a manger.'"

Mae and the angels went to the back again, leaving a perfect picture of the manger scene. The shepherds walked to the front, talking among themselves. Ann held baby Wendell, who was supposed to bleat like a sheep. She hadn't quite learned that animal sound yet.

"We should play a game with these stupid sheep," Oliver suggested. "We have nothing else to do."

Ann gave him a dirty look. "They're not stupid."

"Anyone wanna play a game of Bottoms Up?" Clarke asked.

Merrilyn's eyes became large.

Ralph leaned over and hissed, "They didn't have dice back then."

"Sure they did," Clarke said.

Neena ran to the front and threw her arms above her head. "Hark, ye lowly shepherds."

The shepherds jerked back, surprised.

"Be not afraid," Neena began.

"What's to be afraid of?" Ann asked.

The shepherds giggled.

"Listen to me," Neena shouted. "A baby has been born, a savior for the world. You need to go to Bethlehem and see the baby in the stable."

"Cave," Lou corrected from the back of the church.

Neena put her head in her hand as the crowd laughed.

"Why is he in a cave?" Ann asked.

"Because there was no room in the inn," Neena said.

"Why didn't you make sure there was room if you knew he was coming?" Clarke asked, catching on.

Neena stomped her foot. "Because he had to be born in a cave, okay? Just go see him already."

The shepherds talked among themselves as Mae came to the front once again. "'And suddenly there was with the angel a multitude of the heavenly hosts praising God, and saying, Glory to God in the highest, and on earth peace, goodwill toward men. And it came to pass, as the angels were gone away from them into heaven, the shepherds said one to another, Let us now go even unto Bethlehem, and see this thing which is come to pass, which the Lord hath made known unto us. And they came with haste and found Mary, and Joseph, and the babe lying in a manger.'"

Ruby and the angel choir approached the shepherds. All the kids began singing.

Away in a manger,
no crib for His bed.
The little Lord Jesus
lay down His sweet head.
The stars in the sky
look down where He lay.

The little Lord Jesus
asleep on the hay.
The cattle are lowing,
the poor Baby wakes.
But little Lord Jesus,
no crying He makes.
I love Thee, Lord Jesus,
look down from the sky.
And stay by my side
'til morning is nigh.

The shepherds looked at each other in bewilderment as the angel choir exited.

"I guess we should go see the baby?" Ralph said.

"Yes, we should," Clarke said.

The shepherds walked a whole three feet and were inside the cave. Lillian and Oswald pretended to be surprised at the intrusion.

"We've come to see him," Oliver said.

"You have to be more specific or they'll think we came to see Joseph," Clarke said, jabbing Oliver with his elbow.

"Ow!" Oliver yelped. Glaring at Clarke, he said, "We've come to see the *baby*."

"Baby Jesus," Merrilyn corrected.

"Here he is, in the manger," Lillian said.

"Why is he in the manger?" Ann asked.

"We just *sang* about why he's in a manger, Ann. Weren't you paying attention?" Clarke asked.

Ann glared at him.

Mae opened her Bible again. "Now we skip to Matthew 2. 'Now when Jesus was born in Bethlehem of Judaea in the days of Herod the king, behold, there came wise men from the east to Jerusalem, saying, Where is he that is born King of the Jews? For we have seen his star in the east, and are come to worship him. When Herod the king had heard these things, he was troubled, and all Jerusalem with him. And when he had gathered all the chief priests and scribes of the people together, he demanded of them where Christ should be born. And they said unto him, In Bethlehem of Judaea: for thus it is written by the prophet, and thou Bethlehem, in the land of Juda, art not the least among the princes of Juda: for out of thee shall come a Governor, that shall rule my people Israel.

"'Then Herod, when he had privily called the wise men, enquired of them diligently what time the star appeared. And he sent them to Bethlehem, and said, Go and search diligently for the young child; and when ye have found him, bring me word again, that I may come and worship him also. When they had heard the king, they departed; and, lo, the star, which they saw in the east, went before them, till it came and stood over where the young child was. When they saw the star, they rejoiced with exceeding great joy. And when they were come into the house, they saw the young child with Mary, his mother, and fell down, and worshipped him: and when they had opened their treasures, they presented unto him gifts; gold, and frank-incense, and myrrh. And being warned by God in a dream that they should not return to Herod, they departed into their own country another way."

The three wise men, Belle, Wilbur, and Maggie, walked to the front of the church, carrying rocks as their gifts.

"We've come to visit the King," Belle said in her best 'man voice' that made Neena giggle from the back.

"The King of kings and Lord of lords," Wilbur corrected.

"Well," Lillian hesitated, "Here he is. In the manger."

"A manger!" Maggie exclaimed.

"See? Told ya, Lillian. A manger is no place for a baby," Ann said.

Lillian became slightly pink.

"We present our gifts of gold ... myrrh ... and," Wilbur whispered, "*what was the last one?*"

"Um, myrrh?" Maggie asked.

"I already said that one," Wilbur hissed.

The audience laughed again.

"That concludes our pageant of the first Christmas," Mae said.

There was a wild show of whistles and clapping from the audience while the kids lined up to take their bows. The angels rushed from the back and held hands with their fellow actors. They bowed once, and Reuben fell over.

After laughing, they bowed once more and raced to the back of the church. They had hoped to grab some treats before their mamas could catch them, but the mamas, knowing what the kids would try to do, were already at the table.

FOURTEEN

THE GARDEN AND AN ADDITION

Now IT WAS the spring following that eventful Christmas pageant. The butterflies and insects of the ground began to return from hibernation as the ground recovered from the last winter snow that had fallen in Wildcat Hollow.

Dad had his mind specifically on the hay and wheat crops; he was worried that the latest snow had been too much for them to bear. The kids were going to school five days a week, although Oswald didn't go to school anymore. He stayed with Dad and worked on the farm.

Mama was stir crazy. She always wanted something to do, but ran out of chores every morning before the kids were even off to school. She mended, washed, swept, wiped, cleaned, and dusted every little thing she could think of, but still ran out of things to keep her busy.

Mae, Ruby, Belle, and Lou whispered that it was because she was pregnant again.

"The baby should arrive any time now," Mae whispered when Mama wasn't around.

Seven-year-old Ann stopped her chores and listened to their hushed conversation.

"I hope it's another girl," Belle said.

"We just have to keep Jack's mouth shut," Ruby said.

Lou snickered, "Or he'll ask why she's fat."

Belle hit Lou, which stopped the snickering.

One evening at dinner, Mama and Dad had been discussing things for Mama to do when she was bored, rather jokingly. Without warning, Mama gasped. Dad and the older girls jumped and stared at her in concern.

Mama laughed at their reaction. "Oh, I'm so sorry I startled you. I just had the most wonderful idea of what we could do this weekend that would solve my problem."

"What?" Dad asked.

"We could plant a garden," Mama said, her eyes lighting up.

Dad frowned. "But we already have a garden."

Once again, Mama laughed. "I don't mean a garden for growing food; I mean a garden for growing *flowers*. It's the perfect time to plant summer and fall flowers. You know how much I love Morning Glories, and I heard just this morning that a lady was selling some seeds in town."

Now Dad laughed. "Honey, do you mean to tell me you're gonna get into gardening ..." he looked around the table at the kids and seemed to change his mind about what he was about to say. "Now? You want to become a gardener *now*?"

Mama raised her eyebrows. "You and the kids just make the garden bed, and I'll worry about getting the right seeds."

So on Saturday, the whole family woke early in the morning to start work on the garden bed. The younger kids weren't enthusiastic about giving up their Saturday to build something, but the older ones hushed them by saying that they should do their best to make Mama happy. Mama took the wagon into town and didn't plan on returning until dinner.

The morning was a wonderful one. The sun beamed on the farm, highlighting the little creek with exotic colors. The breeze played with Ann's hair, wisping it about her face like a curious child. The birds chirped and the insects sang; indeed, it was the perfect day to be outside.

Dad gathered his children around him in the backyard. He bent down on his knees in order to be eye level with most of them.

"Today we are going to build Mama's garden," Dad began.

"How are we gonna build the garden?" five-year-old Jack interrupted.

"We're gonna use some of the old wood inside the barn to make a raised bed," Dad explained.

"Oh," Jack said.

"So we need to grab the tools and the wood from the barn. Later we'll grab the manure and soil, but leave it in the barn for now. Got it?" Dad asked.

All the kids nodded their heads "yes" and walked to the barn. Each grabbed a tool and started back to the area Dad claimed would be the garden.

"What is manure?" Jack asked when they got back to the garden.

"Cow poop," Neena said.

Jack fell on the ground with laughter, and Oswald snickered.

"They are so immature," Ruby said to Mae.

Mae nodded her head in agreement.

"And you think you're all that?" Oswald asked, leaning on his gardening hoe.

"Well, I am thirteen now," Ruby reminded him. "And Mae's just turned fourteen. We have moved past the age of laughing at every word Mama deems inappropriate for the supper table."

"You may be fourteen now, but I am more mature than you," Oswald said.

"The fact that you laughed at Neena's remark says otherwise," Mae said.

Oswald raised his eyebrows.

"You know, this would go a lot faster if I had some help. If only I had a bunch of kids. Oh wait, I do," Dad said, dropping an armful of wood.

The kids caught the hint and followed Dad to the barn. When they returned to the proposed garden site, Dad tried to organize them into teams.

"Oswald, Mae, and Ruby should hold the wood since it's heavy. The younger ones can hold the nails for the others, who can hammer *carefully*."

"Do you hammer like this?" Neena asked, hitting the hammer onto the wood.

Chrissa screeched, "You almost smashed my finger!"

"Alright, nevermind," Dad said. "Oswald, Mae, and Ruby, I'll need your help to make the bed. Everyone else, go play."

The kids celebrated and ran off to play.

"Ann, watch Wendell. Make sure she doesn't get into trouble," Dad said.

Ann nodded her head and took Wendell by the hand. "C'mon, Wendell, let's go play in the dirt by the barn."

They walked across the flowing creek towards the barn. There was a little sandy spot near the barn door, perfectly able to hold sand-castles or forts.

Ann and Wendell sat in the dirt, beginning their creative endeavors. They were soon joined by Lou and Jack, whose favorite thing was to get dirty in the sandy spot. Bessie was on the barn swing. Belle was on the gunny sack swing on the tree in the front yard, singing quietly to herself.

On mornings like this, it was quite likely that time would be long forgotten, and what seemed like only a few minutes would end up being a whole morning of playing outside. This is exactly what happened that glorious spring morning, for before Ann knew it, Belle was running from the house to announce Mama's arrival and the command to wash up before dinner.

"How do you like it?" Dad asked Mama after she'd seen it.

"That is the perfect size," Mama said. "And look at all the seeds I bought from the lady in town. She sold me so many!"

"I'm glad you found some. After dinner, we'll fill the bed with manure and dirt so that you can start planting whenever you wish."

"You're the best," Mama said. "You know what else I thought of on my way to town? The Morning Glories have to climb up something to grow."

"What if your Morning Glories climb up the front porch posts so that everyone can see them?" Dad asked. "I'll even make them a special bed out of the leftover wood."

"Oh, you really *are* the best!" Mama exclaimed, throwing her arms around him.

Dad laughed sarcastically. "I really am, aren't I?"

Mama didn't have to worry about what she would do to fill her free time within the next few weeks. Every afternoon when the kids returned from school, they'd always find Mama working in the garden. She worked slowly, but she worked hard nonetheless.

Then one afternoon, the kids came home to find that Mama wasn't in the garden. Dad wasn't out in the wheat field either; the kids could see where he left the tiller. A wagon was parked in the front yard.

They must have guests, Ann thought.

They skipped to the house and were just about to storm inside when Oswald ran out.

"Hush!" He spat. They hushed. "Mama's having her baby and Mrs. Phillips said no one can talk while they're inside. Dad says go play and he'll call you when the baby's here."

There was a moment of stunned silence. The older girls beamed while the younger kids looked on in confusion.

"A *baby*?" Jack asked. "Mama's having a *baby*?"

"Now? *Right now*?" Bessie asked.

"Yes, that's what I just told you," Oswald said, exasperated.

"When did this happen?" Jack asked, looking appalled at the fact that he didn't know sooner.

"No more questions. Go play before Dad comes out here," Oswald warned.

The kids dropped their school books on the porch and raced away. They played outside the whole rest of the afternoon and part of the evening. About the time that they were getting hungry for supper, Mrs. Phillips left and Dad called them for dinner. Whippoorwill peas and cornbread were dealt out for the kids to eat at the table on the porch.

"Once you eat your food, you can go see your new brother," he said.

"A brother?" Ann asked.

"Another boy!" Oswald said, raising his hands in the air triumphantly.

Oswald and Jack danced around the table in delight. The kids gulped down their supper in their excitement to meet the newest member of the Bennett family.

In five minutes, everyone had finished their bowl of peas. Dad made them line up and quietly opened the door to his bedroom. There Mama lay in bed with the newest Bennett child, a boy, whom they named Leon.

The girls fawned over him and passed him around, cooing over his tiny face and little hands. Oswald and Jack talked about who would be the one to teach him hunting, fishing, talking, swimming, walking, swinging, and other activities boys enjoyed doing.

Mama and Dad watched their kids, now *twelve* of them, and smiled with pure joy.

FIFTEEN

MAMA'S GONE AND DAD'S IN CHARGE

JUNE 1940

I was a nice summer afternoon in 1940. The new baby, Leon, was no longer a baby; he was a bright, happy, talkative, and very mischievous little one-year-old. Wendell was almost three, and Jack was six. Ann had just turned nine, and Bessie was about to turn nine in a few days. Neena was nine, Chrissa was almost eleven (and proud of it), Lou and Belle were both thirteen, Ruby was fourteen, Mae was fifteen, and Oswald was eighteen.

And so on this nice summer afternoon, Mama had planned to make a cake for Bessie's birthday. All the kids were playing outside except for Chrissa and Wendell, who were using Mama's old magazines to make paper dolls on the dining room table.

Mama was inside stirring the cake batter when Bessie, Ann, and Jack walked inside, all looking very serious.

"Well, what is this about?" Mama asked, stopping her stirring.

"We want to ask a question," Ann said.

"What is it?" Mama asked, curious because she knew this "question" could be about anything.

"Ellen said that we're coming out of a ... what was it?" Bessie asked.

"A dep ... deprison?" Ann asked.

Mama chuckled. "Depression?"

"Yeah," they said together.

"Is that true?" Bessie asked.

"Well ... yes," Mama said, rather hesitantly.

"What is it?" Jack asked, sticking his finger up his nose.

"A depression is when the country doesn't have a lot of money, and so the families don't have a lot of money."

"Why were we in it?" Ann asked.

"Well, there was a sudden drop in the economy. Everything became cheaper."

Bessie frowned, "But we like that."

"Well, normally we would, but it became so cheap that everyone lost money at the same time."

"Oh," Bessie said.

"Do we have more money now?" Ann asked.

"Kinda."

"Are we rich?" Jack asked, his eyes growing wide.

"No, not rich," Mama laughed.

"Then why are you making a cake? I thought it was expensive to make a cake," Ann said, peeking over the mixing bowl.

"To celebrate Bessie's birthday," Mama smiled.

Jack smiled slyly. "Can I taste the cake batter?"

Mama grinned. "If you want any of this cake you better get on outta the kitchen."

The three kids ran outside, giggling as Mama popped the kitchen towel after them.

Ann stopped on the porch and collapsed onto a rocking chair. *I hope we have the cake tonight.* She started when Dad ran onto the porch, laughing hard. *Mama must've chased him out of the kitchen with a towel too,* Ann giggled.

A wagon came into sight down their road. Ann squinted, trying to see who it was. Dad leaned into the house and announced the wagon to Mama. Mama walked out onto the porch, wiping her floury hands on her apron.

"Why would Carrie come to visit so late in the afternoon?" Mama asked, stepping off the porch to meet Carrie as the wagon stopped.

"Amerie, come quick!" Carrie exclaimed, jumping off the wagon.

"What is it?" Mama asked, bewildered.

"It's Thelma. Thelma Caldwell," Carrie gasped. "She's gone into labor, and Ethel can't help with the delivery. She sent Ralph to ask me to help and I just knew I wouldn't be able to deliver the baby myself since Thelma is so petite. Oh, you must come quick!"

The kids had gathered around, hoping to see the Phillips kids, but to no avail.

Mama untied her apron with lightning-quick hands while giving Dad instructions. "Get the cake out of the oven and frost it, and then cover it with something to keep the flies off of it. Make supper for the kids, there's stuff in the cellar to make stew. Leon is asleep but he will wake up in a few minutes, so get him up and play with him until supper. Everyone needs to be in bed by nine."

She climbed into the wagon beside Carrie, tossing her apron down to Dad, who caught it. "I'll be back as soon as I can, but this could take all night."

Carrie started the wagon with a jolt, and they went down the lane, leaving only a trail of dust, some slurred instructions, and a flustered Dad.

The kids watched the wagon silently, and when it was gone, they shrugged their shoulders and went back to playing around the farm. Ruby walked inside, murmuring about the cake, and Mae followed to take care of supper. Dad stood in the front yard, still processing what had happened.

He finally walked inside the house and clapped his hands together. He stood in the doorway, as if he didn't exactly know what to do with this new level of responsibility.

"You've never been left alone with everyone before, have you?" Mae asked.

Dad smiled. "Nope. How much you wanna bet she'll send someone to check on us?"

"That will probably happen," Ruby laughed.

"I do not doubt it," Mae said.

There was a faint cry from the bedroom, and Dad snapped his fingers with realization. He brought Leon out of the bedroom and into the kitchen.

"This is our chance, Leon. Mama's gone and Dad's in charge. What are we gonna do?" Dad asked, bouncing Leon in his arms. He thought about his question, then directed it to Mae and Ruby. "What exactly did she say?"

"Frost and store the cake, eat supper, play with Leon, go to bed by nine," Mae said.

"I'm glad you caught that. I couldn't understand a word she said. She was speaking so fast."

"We got it, Dad," Mae assured him. "You can go play with Leon, and we'll take care of the cake and supper."

"Really? Can you girls do it on your own?" Dad asked.

Ruby grinned. "Dad, I'm fourteen and Mae's fifteen. I think we got this."

Dad grinned back. "I'll be right outside if you need me."

Neena, Chrissa, and Belle were fighting over the gunny sack swing. Ann, Wendell, Jack, and Bessie were playing in the sandy spot near the barn. Lou was on the barn swing, and Oswald was stroking Clover, his new horse, and feeding her hay.

Leon clapped his hands and reached towards the ground. Dad stepped off the porch and set him in the dirt, where he made his way towards the sandy spot.

"Dad!" some of the kids exclaimed when they noticed he was outside. They gathered around him, wondering if he wanted to play with him.

"We could play 'run, sheep, run,'" Neena suggested.

"I absolutely refuse to run," Chrissa objected.

"How about tag?" Belle asked.

Jack exclaimed, "Pirate ship!"

"No, let's play 'house' in the barn," Bessie said.

"House is boring. Let's make a fort in the field," Lou said.

Dad's eyes were wide by this point. "Maybe we could find a game everyone likes?"

Ann shot her hand in the air. "What about hide-and-go-seek?"

The kids agreed.

"You have to be it first, Ann," Lou said.

"Count to twenty-five," Belle said.

"Close your eyes," Neena reminded her.

The kids ran off, spreading the word to those who hadn't heard as Ann started counting. Dad looked around, chuckled to himself, and ran towards the barn, picking up Leon as he went.

They played a few rounds of hide-and-go-seek until Mae came out of the house, announcing supper.

"Oh well," Dad said. "We could play again after dinner."

"And that would be fun in the dark," Lou said.

The kids stormed inside the house to scarf down dinner and prepare for another game.

"This time, we could hide anywhere 'cause it'll be dark," Belle said.

"I know exactly where I'm hiding," Lou said.

"I don't think I will play," Chrissa said. "It's too dark."

Dinner was served and devoured within minutes, and the excitement over playing hide-and-go-seek in the dark never died away.

Bessie noticed the frosted cake on the counter. "Are we eating that tonight?"

"We should wait until Mama is home," Ruby said.

"We'll eat it tomorrow," Mae said. "Cake is always better the second day, anyway."

Bessie looked down, and Dad changed the subject.

"I bet that *I'll* be the last one Neena finds in hide-and-seek," he said, walking down the porch steps.

The kids jumped out of their chairs and hurried after him, squealing and giggling at the idea of playing hide-and-seek in the dark.

"We'll leave the house lamps on so that we can at least see a little bit," Dad said.

"What are the rules?" Mae asked.

"You have to hide in the front or back yards; no going into the fields," Neena said.

"The house is base, and you have to tag us before we get there," Lou said.

"If we play it like that, then I will need another seeker," Neena said.

"Who do you want?" Ann asked.

Neena pointed to Bessie. "I want Bessie to be a seeker with me."

Bessie shrugged her shoulders.

"Are we playing when you're tagged you're a seeker too?" Mae asked.

"Yeah," Ann said.

"And you can't run to base until a seeker has been near your hiding spot," Belle said.

Lou shrugged, "That sounds fair."

"Okay, we'll say the front porch is base, and you can't run to it until a seeker has been near your hiding spot," Dad said.

"I'm not running to base, but I'll hide," Oswald said.

"Fair enough," Mae said.

It's because of his left leg, Ann thought.

"Now Bessie and Neena, close your eyes and count to twenty. Actually, count to forty since it's really dark," Ruby said.

Neena and Bessie squeezed their eyes shut and began counting. All the others ran off into the dark. Ann stood for a moment in the front yard, trying to decide what would be the best hiding place. She knew the barn would be thoroughly searched, so she decided against it. Lou and Belle were already in the tree, so she decided not to join them either.

She hadn't seen anyone go to the backyard yet. And there was a tree with a branch she could easily reach. And since the tree was in the back, the light from the front porch wouldn't reach.

Ann grinned to herself as she sprinted around the house. She heard Neena shout "forty!" but she knew they wouldn't come to the back for a while. She caught hold of the branch and climbed up the trunk until she was sitting cross-legged on the branch. She could see just a little from the light coming through the kitchen window.

There was a shout, a scream, and giggles from the front yard. Leaves rustled around, and someone fell with a grunt. A distorted shout of "let's go to the barn," echoed around the little farmhouse.

They must have caught Belle and Lou.

It was quiet for a few minutes. Then screams filled the air, along with a string of laughter from Oswald.

He must have scared them, Ann laughed to herself.

She heard footsteps coming around the house. She leaned closer to the tree as Bessie and Lou rounded the corner and looked around in the darkness. Ann could just barely make out their shadowy figures inching along the house.

"Anyone back here?" Bessie asked in a shrill whisper.

Lou hissed. "If someone was back here, they wouldn't own up to it."

An owl hooted in the distance, stopping Bessie from responding.

Lou stood for a moment longer and then scoffed. "No one's back here. It's too dark. C'mon, let's go back to the barn."

They turned and walked back around the house. Ann waited a second before climbing slowly out of the tree. She slipped around the other side of the house, stopping near the front to get a good look at where everyone was. Ann was hidden in the shadows, so she knew no one could see her.

Lou and Bessie were near the front porch, looking around for people trying to sneak to base. Chrissa and Leon were sitting on the porch, watching. From the sound of it, Neena and Belle were trying to muster their courage to walk into the pitch-black barn.

They'll never be able to go into the dark barn again.

A scream was heard from the barn. Lou and Bessie looked over and then started walking towards the barn. When they had disappeared into the shadows, Ann raced out of her hiding spot.

Lou hadn't gone as far as Bessie and saw exactly when Ann jumped around the corner of the house. An epic chase occurred, resulting in Ann reaching the porch just a little bit before Lou brushed her back with her hand.

"Gotcha!" Lou yelled.

"No, I got to base first," Ann said, gasping for breath.

"No, I tagged you first," Lou said.

"You aren't even it, Lou," Ann retorted.

"Yes I am," Lou said. "I've been tagged."

Another shout was heard from the barn.

"We found 'em," Neena screamed.

The sound of a stampede grew louder until all the people who hadn't yet been found burst into the light, trying to reach the porch. Bessie and Lou scrambled to tag everyone. Neena and Belle came panting behind the crowd, who were a jumble of giggles, gasps, and laughter.

Dad plopped onto the porch stairs, gasping for air while he laughed. The others sat too, each trying to catch their breath. After a minute, the sound of heavy breathing had gone away.

"Y'all wanna play another round?" Dad asked.

"Yeah!" they all shouted.

"Lou and Belle are it this time," Neena said.

"Hide!" Ruby shouted.

And so they all scattered, and the game began again. They played another three games before Dad walked inside to check the time. He came running out, looking slightly terrified.

"It's almost ten o'clock!" he shouted.

The kids gasped.

"Hurry, go inside and get ready for bed," Ruby said.

Everyone ran inside and scrambled for pajamas, hairbrushes, and a chance inside the outhouse. It should have been a world record; all twelve of the kids were in their beds in the living room and kitchen within twenty minutes. And not a minute too soon, for a wagon was heard coming back up the driveway soon afterward.

"Everyone hush and go to sleep," Dad said to the kids as they snuggled under their blankets. "Don't say anything to Mama, and don't open your eyes, or she'll see that you're awake."

Ann snuggled underneath the quilt next to Bessie. Neena and Chrissa slept on the opposite end of the bed. Ann kept her eyes open just a little to see what would happen.

Dad smoothed his hair and did his best to clean the kitchen from supper. All the dishes had been left on the table, forgotten until now. When Mama walked inside, Dad was whistling as he washed the dishes.

"Well, hi there," Dad said, pretending to be taken by surprise.

"Hi," Mama said.

"How's the baby?"

"He's a perfect little angel. His name is George. And his mother issei's perfectly fine as well." Mama said. "How were the kids?"

"Oh, just fine," Dad said. "We played hide-and-go-seek."

"Oh, you did?" Mama asked, casting a confused glance at the dishes he was still washing.

"Yes. And we had supper, and we left the cake so that you can enjoy it with us."

Mama smiled. "You didn't have to do that."

"It was the kids' idea, not mine," Dad said. "I tried to eat it tonight, but the kids made me wait."

Mama laughed.

Bessie giggled beside Ann.

Mama raised her eyebrows at Dad, who was trying his best to pretend he hadn't heard anything.

"Lonzo," Mama began.

Dad's in soooo much trouble.

"Is there something you want to tell me?" Mama asked, crossing her arms.

"Yes," Dad said after a moment's hesitation. "Hide-and-go-seek is quite fun with the children. You should try it sometime."

Ann tried not to smile and covered her head with the quilt. Neena was shaking with silent laughter, and Bessie giggled out loud *again*.

Mama shook her head and laughed. "Well, maybe I will." She leaned forward and kissed him on the cheek. "I'm going to get ready for bed. Finish the dishes and blow out the lamps before you come to bed."

"Alright, honey," Dad said as she walked to the bedroom.

Mama stopped at the doorway. "And make sure to tell the kids that tonight was the only night they get to stay up. From now on, I'll be home to make sure they get tucked into bed on time."

A chorus of "Aww!"s rang about the house. Dad sighed and put his head in his hands, and Mama laughed as she walked into the bedroom.

SIXTEEN

THE DANCE AND THE COURTSHIP

"WHERE IS MY PRETTY PINK RIBBON?" Chrissa yelled.

"I need my hat," Lou shouted. "Where is my hat? Did you take my hat?"

"Who hid my shoe? I put it right underneath the chair and now it's gone," Bessie said.

These were the sounds escaping the house when Dad walked inside for his dinner. He raised his eyebrows. "Sounds like you've been having a blast," he said, kissing Mama on the forehead.

"The fun is just beginning," Mama said as she set his dinner on the table.

More shouts and giggles echoed around the house.

Dad couldn't help but laugh. "They're a little excited for the party tonight, aren't they?"

"Just a little," Mama chuckled.

"I need my shoe," Bessie yelled again.

"Who hid my purple hat? Was it you, Jack?" Lou asked accusingly.

"I can't find my brush anywhere," Mae said.

"I *need* my pink ribbon!" Chrissa shouted with emphasis.

"Found my brush," Mae said, holding it above her head.

"Here's your pink ribbon, Chrissa. It was in my shoe," Belle said, holding up the coveted ribbon.

"Scooch, Mae, I need to use the mirror," Ann said, shoving Mae.

"My hat!" Lou called in distress. "Has anyone seen it?"

"Here's my shoe," Bessie said.

Oswald groaned as he pulled his work shoes on. "Why are there so many *ribbons* in this house?

"You have to share the mirror!" Ann screamed.

"I *am* sharing. You're just taking more of your share," Mae protested.

"Where is my - oh, found it," Lou said, pulling her lost purple hat from underneath some rumpled quilts.

"*Again* with the ribbons," Oswald scoffed, stepping over a pile of assorted colored ribbons.

Dad laughed. "We may as well admit that we're outnumbered, Oswald. There will *always* be ribbons in this house."

Mama laughed at the comment as Dad and Oswald walked to the fields to finish the workday.

They had been looking forward to the party since August when Mama and Dad had finally agreed that they could have one. Invitations were sent out the first week of November because the girls were worried someone would not be able to make it. In the week leading up to the dance, the girls had done nothing but talk about it around the kitchen table while Mama listened with amused interest.

And now, the day of the party, the girls were the most excited they'd ever been. The whole afternoon was spent in preparation for the party. The younger girls cleaned up their ribbon mess; Mae, Ruby, and Belle helped bake the desserts; and the others set about cleaning what Mama told them to around the farm.

The party would start around five o'clock. The guests would arrive, snacks and cakes would be placed on the porch table, and then the dancing would begin as soon as everyone had arrived. The girls, in their anticipation of the first arrivals, waited on the front porch, eyes peeled for any sign of movement down the driveway.

"Get off my dress or you'll wrinkle it," Chrissa scolded Bessie.

"Move your dress so I can sit too," Bessie said, pushing Chrissa's dress out of the way.

Chrissa shrieked and swatted at Bessie.

Mae pursed her lips and gave each a look of disapproval.

"Quit arguing or you'll be sent to your room during the party," Belle hissed.

"And you won't be able to dance with the boys," Ruby said before Lou jabbed her in the rib.

The girls squealed with laughter.

"Dad says we aren't allowed to dance with the boys by ourselves," Belle said.

"Dad was just kidding like always," Neena protested.

"Mama agreed with him," Ann said. "So he probably wasn't joking."

"You're only ten, Ann, so of course *you* can't dance with the boys," Ruby said.

"Ellen and Jeanette were allowed to dance with boys at *their* party," Ann retorted, flouncing her dress and sitting on the porch with a sigh.

"Ellen and Jeanette are spoiled," Neena protested.

"They've never worked a day in their life," Lou said, crossing her arms.

"Girls, don't be mean," Ruby said.

"It's the truth," Ann grumbled.

"Look! Someone's coming down the driveway," Bessie shouted, jumping off of the porch and onto the grass below.

The girls shrieked and followed Bessie off the porch. They paused for a moment before Lou groaned, "Oh, Bessie, you tricked us. How could you be so cruel?"

"It was just a leaf," Belle said, disappointed.

"I didn't do it on purpose," Bessie protested.

They sat back down on the porch, swinging their legs over the newly cut grass. They broke off into chatter of who was surely coming, who couldn't make it, and who they were looking forward to being with. Soon, another false alarm was cried out, but it turned out to be Dad and Oswald coming back from the field. The girls expressed their disappointment adamantly, to the disapproval of the boys.

Ann frowned, hushing the girls around her.

I thought I heard wagons' wheels down the dirt road.

"Do ... y'all hear that?" she asked hesitantly.

The girls hushed and listened. The sound grew louder and louder until a wagon rumbled around the corner and into sight. The girls stood on the porch to whoop and cheer the arrival of the first wagon.

Ann ran back inside for just a moment to tell Mama that the Phillips were here. Dad stood abruptly and walked into the bedroom, mumbling about needing to change clothes. Mama and Oswald both smoothed their hair and waited for the guests to be ushered into the living room.

The Phillips were heartily welcomed into the house. Desserts were shown off and dresses were admired, like normal. The Chinx family arrived, and then the Kanili family, and then Ralph Poher, bringing along a friend, Gilbert Raslo.

Gilbert was an entertaining young man who enjoyed making others laugh. He was eighteen and apprenticing under Wildcat Hollow's only carpenter. He only had eight and a half fingers because of a farming accident, but he'd grown used to living life without the first three fingers on his right hand.

Soon the little house was bustling with guests in their best dancing attire, drooling over the desserts and chattering about petty life issues. Oswald and Lillian had found their way to the dining chairs and were talking and laughing together. Every person in the room secretly hoped they would end up together, but not even their own mothers knew if they liked each other.

The eldest of the Bennett girls had found company with Ralph and his guest, Gilbert. The boys were masters at flattery, and the girls were taken by the mysterious boy before the first song had been played. Ruby seemed especially to like Gilbert, directing all her questions and comments to him at every possible moment. Dad looked on with suspicion, but Mama laughed and told him to lighten up.

Mr. Chinx brought his harmonica and Mr. Kanili had his dulcimer, and together they played the folk-songs of the day. Dad clapped along to the rhythm while Mama sang the lyrics.

When the first song was played, the whole group gathered in the front yard to dance. After that, the mothers quit dancing and sat on the porch, snacking and talking. Ann danced with the other kids until her feet hurt. They collapsed onto the porch to enjoy refreshments and the setting sun.

Ruby was sitting near Gilbert on the porch. He looked at her for a moment, and she blushed and turned towards the setting sun.

Ew! He touched her hand, Ann thought as she watched them talk. She shuddered in disgust and redirected her attention to Merrilyn and Maggie. *I hope that more dancing will happen soon.*

Dad walked outside to announce the beginning of another batch of songs. The kids cheered and skipped out into the front yard, followed by Dad after he looked long and hard at Gilbert and Ruby.

The night was finished with another round of dancing, singing, and cheerfulness. At a time Mama called "way past your bedtime," the guests left, and the kids were sent to bed, each bubbling over with the excitement from the party. It took quite a few demands from Mama to quiet the girls enough to go to sleep.

The next morning, the girls were helping with the cleanup of the party when a wagon rumbled up the driveway again. The girls ran to the door but couldn't figure out who was driving the wagon. Dad walked outside to meet their guest but came back inside to announce that Gilbert requested to see Ruby.

Ruby hurried to the mirror to fix her hair before walking outside to meet Gilbert. The other girls tried to listen at the window with

Dad, but Mama put a stop to that and sent them to finish their chores. She couldn't stop the girls from whispering, however, and boy, how they whispered.

Multiple rumors had been spread before Ruby bounced inside, face flushed, telling Dad that Gilbert wanted to see him. Dad raised his eyebrow and walked outside. Ruby was immediately surrounded by her sisters, who demanded to know what Gilbert had said. This time Mama did not try to stop them but listened closely as she pretended to wash the dishes.

"He wanted to know if I would court him," Ruby said.

The girls shrieked.

"What did you say?" Mae asked.

"I told him I would, but he had to ask Dad's permission first."

The girls squealed again. Mama reappeared from the kitchen, looking proud and sad at the same time.

"But Ruby's only sixteen," Bessie protested.

"Mama was sixteen when she married Dad," Belle said. Then she saw Mama's curious look. "Not you, Mama, but our other Mama."

"Will Dad agree?" Ann asked.

Ruby looked at Mama for the answer.

"He might," Mama shrugged.

As if on cue, Dad walked inside. "Gilbert's outside, Ruby."

Ruby planted a kiss on Dad's cheek and walked out the front door.

"What did you say?" the girls immediately asked. Mama looked at him expectantly.

"Well, I guess we now have a grown woman in our family. I've allowed the courtship," he said.

All the girls screamed their delight, causing poor Leon to cry.

An hour later Ruby walked inside, as if on a cloud, after seeing Gilbert off.

SEVENTEEN

THE WAR AND SHARECROPPING

JULY WAS DUSTY, dry, and hot. Very hot. But that didn't stop the cotton from growing. Since the kids were out of school for the summer, and the war was plaguing the nation, they tried to help Mama and Dad earn extra money however they could. Early in the morning, they would get up and walk a mile to the "Big Man's" house. The Big Man grew cotton and allowed the kids to pick it for a share of the profit.

The first morning, all eight girls were walking down the dirt road to the Big Man's house when the subject of the war came up.

"Why didn't Dad get drafted for the war?" Ann asked as she skipped along.

"Because he's much too old," Ruby said.

"Why wasn't Oswald drafted, then? He's not too old," Bessie said.

"Oswald has a limp," Mae explained. "They won't let him fight."

"That's rude," Neena said.

"He was glad about it," Belle said.

"So was Mama," Chrissa added.

"Gilbert can't fight either," Ruby said.

"If he had all ten fingers he could," Lou snickered.

Ruby jabbed her in the ribs.

Ann tried not to giggle at the comment as she continued down the road. Ever since war had been declared, one thought had plagued her mind. *When will the war be over?*

There was a moment of silence before Bessie asked what Ann was thinking.

"Could be anytime," Belle said. "Could be tomorrow or ten years from now."

"Let's hope for tomorrow," Ann said.

They rounded a corner and stopped short, jaws dropped as they stared at the Big Man's house. It was a two-story building, with four flower gardens in the front yard alone. The large windows were framed with green shutters, and a porch extended the length of the front. White columns lined the front porch as dozens of plants hung from the porch ceiling.

The girls tiptoed up the porch steps and knocked on the door.

"What's that?" Neena asked, pointing to a round knob beside the door.

"Something fancy, I guess," Mae said.

"Press it," Lou said.

"Don't," Mae warned, but it was too late.

Neena pressed it, and it rang.

"It sounds like a bell," Ann said.

The door was opened by a fine gentleman in a nice black suit. "Are you the Bennett children?"

"Yes, sir," Mae answered.

The man eyed each of them carefully.

"You going somewhere, Mister? It ain't church day if that's where you were going," Neena said.

"Neena," Mae scolded.

Ruby introduced herself and stuck out her hand.

The man raised an eyebrow before shaking her hand slightly.

"And I'm Jack. Come inside. The Misses will see you soon," he said, stepping aside.

"My brother's named -" Lou's voice trailed off as she entered the hallway.

Huge paintings hung on the walls, lining the long hallway. Priceless treasures of gold and silver stood on fancy glass pedestals. One large chandelier hung from the ceiling that seemed to be as far up as the sky itself.

"Don't touch anything, and follow me," Jack said, walking briskly down the hallway.

The kids gaped at the fancy patterned carpet and smooth walls. They entered the Big Man's living room and were told to wait while Jack went to get the Misses. The kids continued to gape around them, admiring the ornate furniture and beautifully framed windows.

Jack re-entered the living room. "The Misses will be here momentarily."

"Is she lost?" Ann asked.

"No, the Misses is not lost," he said in his slow drawl.

"I'd get lost in this big house," Bessie whispered to Chrissa, who nodded in agreement.

"Where does the Big Man sleep? I don't see a bed in here," Neena said, looking around.

"He does not sleep in here," Jack said.

"Then does he sleep in the kitchen?" Ann asked, craning her neck to try and catch a glimpse of the forbidden area.

Jack sighed. "No. He sleeps in his bedroom."

"Oh."

A middle-aged woman with streaks of gray in her hair walked into the living room from one of the many hallways and greeted the children warmly. She handed them each a sack that was taller than them. "Here you are, girls. If you fill this whole sack up with cotton, you get a whole quarter. *A whole quarter.* But you have to fill the whole sack."

"Yes, Ma'am. We will, Ma'am," Ruby said.

The girls were guided out of the house and into the cotton fields. Many other people were picking cotton, but the girls were led to an empty field that had not been touched. They were instructed on how to pick out the cotton

They walked down the rows of cotton, picking out the white tufts and tossing them into their long sacks. The heads of the stems poked at their fingers, making them bleed.

Ann and Bessie began complaining after working for an hour.

"We have to keep working to earn our quarter," Mae said as she kept picking cotton.

"But I'm so tired," Ann complained.

"Mama always says to sing, and the work will go faster," Belle said.

"That's a great idea," Ruby said.

"What song, then?" Bessie asked.

"Let's sing *Rock of Ages*," Chrissa said.

Lou groaned, "No, we *always* sing that one. I can never get it out of my head."

"Let's do one with an echo," Ruby said.

Neena nodded, "Yeah, those are more fun."

Ann thought for a moment. "How about *In The Sweet By and By*. That one has an echo."

The girls agreed and began singing. Mae, Belle, Neena, and Ann sang the first part while Ruby, Chrissa, Lou, and Bessie sang the echo.

There's a land that is fairer than day,
And by faith we can see it afar;
For the father waits over the way
To prepare us a dwelling place there.
In the sweet (in the sweet)
By and by (by and by),
We shall meet on that beautiful shore;

In the sweet (in the sweet)
By and by (by and by),
We shall meet on that beautiful shore.

They worked and sang in this way until dinner.

Underneath the shade of the Big Man's oak trees, they ate the dinner Mama had packed for them. They talked about many different things, the war being a prominent subject. A prayer was said for Hudson, their oldest brother, and Jack, Ellie's husband, who had been drafted and sent overseas already.

After dinner, they returned to picking cotton. Mae and Ruby were the first to fill their sacks, with Lou as a close third. After handing in their sacks and receiving their quarters, they helped the younger girls fill their own sacks. When all of the bags were filled to the brim, around supper time, they each brought home a quarter for Mama.

EIGHTEEN

THE ENGAGEMENT AND THE NEWS

SEPTEMBER - NOVEMBER 1942

It was a wonderful Autumn day in September of 1942. The wind was billowing around playfully, shaking the branches and leaves of the trees. It had been a very rainy start to the week, but today showed a promise of sunshine and warmth.

Mama was expecting another baby, Ann knew. Of course, Mama hadn't announced it to the kids, but her baby bump was getting larger by the day. The older girls whispered bets about if it would be a girl or a boy. The younger kids were oblivious to what was happening.

All the kids except for Leon were off to school, having just started the new school year. This would be Ruby and Mae's last year at the little one-room schoolhouse; a bitter-sweet time for everyone.

Mama and Dad were anxious for the kids to get back. There was a major family discussion that needed to happen, but they refused to give any hints to Oswald before the rest of the kids were there. Oswald was perfectly fine with it, for he had a secret that needed to be shared too.

The stomping of feet on the front porch announced the arrival of the kids. The front door burst open, and the giggling and chatter of the children filled the house instantly. Mud was half-heartedly shaken off of shoes before they were carried into the house and placed in their designated corner. Mama put down her dishes for only a moment, before sighing and picking them up again.

"Did you hear, Mama?" Lou asked, bubbling over with excitement.

"What?" Mama said.

"Oliver likes Lou," Belle said with the least enthusiasm, flopping onto a bed.

"The whole school knows because Wilbur is a secret-spiller," Ann said.

"Ann, that's not nice," Mama scolded.

"Oh, it's true, Mama. Wilbur can't keep a secret for nothing," Neena said.

"Well, that may be true, but it doesn't mean you have to say that behind his back," Mama said.

"Oh, but Mama," Lou said dramatically. "It doesn't matter who said what. Oliver likes me!" And with that, she flung herself on her bed.

Neena rolled her eyes while Mama looked on in amusement. Dad walked in to find Ann laughing at Lou.

"What's going on here?" he asked.

"Lou has a suitor," Chrissa said, tossing her curled hair.

"Oh *really*?" Dad asked, spinning to face Lou. "And who might this be?"

Lou blushed. "Oliver."

"Oliver who?"

"Kanili, Dad," Lou said, knowing he was teasing.

"Hmmm," Dad stroked his chin. "Nice family. I'm not so sure about the boy, however."

Five-year-old Wendell giggled and jumped on him. "You're just kidding, Dad."

Dad grinned, "No, I'm completely serious."

Wendell giggled again and ran outside.

"But seriously, Lou, he better keep away from you."

Lou grinned and then stopped. She shrugged, flipped off the bed, and followed Wendell outside.

Mama pulled Dad into the kitchen and began speaking in a low whisper.

Ann and Neena glanced at each other and smiled mischievously. They crawled underneath the blankets on their bed to listen.

"When will we tell them?" Mama asked.

"After supper," Dad replied quietly. "We don't want to spoil the family supper."

"How will they take the news?"

"There will be many tears, I fear."

Neena rustled underneath the blankets.

"*Shhh*," Ann hissed. "*Be still.*"

Dad noticed the two girl-shaped lumps underneath the blankets and clasped his hands together. "Yes, I'm sorry, but we will have to wait until after supper to tell Ann and Neena that we must sell their toys for food," he said, raising his voice so the girls could clearly hear him.

"Dad!" Neena cried, throwing back the blankets.

"You won't," Ann said.

"Oh, I won't, will I?" Dad asked, chasing the girls as they squealed around the living room and into his bedroom.

There was a knock on the door, and Bessie raced to get it.

"It's Gilbert, Ruby," Bessie yelled, bending over backward to shout the news.

"I, um, actually wasn't here to see Ruby, Bessie," Gilbert said, clearing his throat. "I'm actually here to talk to your father."

Dad walked out of the bedroom and guided his visitor to the front porch. When Dad walked back inside with Gilbert, supper was already on the table.

They were out there for a long time, Ann thought.

Ruby and Gilbert greeted each other, and Gilbert was asked to stay for supper. Gilbert agreed but said he had some urgent business with Ruby that needed to happen first.

So Gilbert once again walked outside, this time followed timidly by Ruby. Dad gave Mama a knowing look, and a silent tear slipped down her cheek. They watched Gilbert and Ruby leave the front yard and walk into the pasture.

When Gilbert and Ruby returned, supper was almost finished by the rest of the family.

"We have big news," Gilbert said as they sat down.

The clanking of the silverware stopped momentarily as they all turned to face Gilbert and Ruby.

"We're getting married," Ruby said with a burst of excitement.

It was as if a volcano of happiness erupted right there at the table. All the girls hugged and giggled while the boys gathered around Gilbert to congratulate him. Ruby, Mama, Mae, and Belle cried.

Ann raised her eyebrows. *Why are they crying? This is a happy moment, right?*

After the chaotic happiness died down, Mama glanced over at Oswald and realized something was wrong.

"You okay, Oswald?" she asked, wiping her tears.

"Yeah," he said to his plate.

"Well, you don't look okay," Mama said.

Oswald chuckled. "I had something to tell you guys after dinner, but I don't want to spoil their happy moment. I'll wait until tomorrow."

Lou rolled her eyes. "Well, now we wanna know, genius."

The rest of the table chorused in agreement.

"Well, okay," Oswald began, taking his hands off of the table and setting them in his lap. "Lillian and I have been courting for only a little while." He stopped to clear his throat. "But we've decided that marriage is the way we should go. I am going to ask for her mother's permission this weekend."

Another cheer erupted from the table. Mama's tears were flowing freely now, as two of her children were to be engaged in the same week. People thumped each other on the back, and it was a rather enjoyable end to the evening meal.

But after the evening meal came the hard news, Mama and Dad knew. Gilbert thanked them for dinner, kissed Ruby goodbye, and left. After his departure, Mama and Dad sat all the kids in the living room.

"It's been a fun evening. An exciting evening for everyone. And Mama and I could not be happier for you guys," Dad began, giving Ruby and Oswald a nod. He took a breath before continuing. "But now we have some bad news. We have more than the amount of homesteading land allotted to each family, but most of the land is not able to be farmed. We do not produce enough crops to feed fourteen people."

Almost fifteen people, Ann thought, with a look at Mama's growing belly.

"We have to move somewhere where there's more farmland," Dad said.

There was a gasp, and everyone began protesting at once.

"Calm down," Dad shouted above the chatter. "We know how hard this will be on our family, so trust us. We will not be making this decision lightly."

"My wedding," Ruby moaned.

"We won't move until you and Gilbert are properly married, Ruby," Mama comforted her.

"Where will Lillian and I live?" Oswald asked.

"Surely you weren't thinking of Lillian and yourself living with us after you are married?" Dad asked.

"Well," Oswald threw his hands up in frustration. "We haven't gotten that far."

"Oliver and I won't see each other," Lou said.

"Merrilyn!" Ann gasped.

"The treehouse won't be able to come with us," Jack said, shocked.

"Mama won't be able to come with us," Belle whispered.

Her Mama, Lonzo's first wife, had been buried on their land. Belle was right. She would not be making the trip.

"Obviously we all need some time to think this over," Dad said, clearing his throat.

Ann heard the emotion through his voice anyway.

"Let's just stick the matter out of our heads and do something else with the rest of the evening. We'll reassess in the morning. Goodnight." And with that, Dad left the room.

Everyone shortly followed to their own beds, but none slept very well that night. The next morning was not a particularly happy morning. Bleary eyes and croaking voices attended the breakfast table while eggs, sausage, and fresh biscuits were passed around.

"So, how did everyone sleep?" Mama asked in a weak voice.

Some grumbles, mutters, and whispers answered.

Dad became angry. "Don't you guys understand what is at stake here? We have to move away because otherwise, we will starve. Do you want to starve?"

The kids stared at him, wide-eyed. No one said a word.

"I didn't think so. So quit your grumbling and let's have a nice family breakfast."

Belle was openly crying again, along with some of the younger ones. Ann returned her attention to her plate. Her appetite was gone.

Dad exhaled and ran his hand over his hair. "Sorry. That - I shouldn't have said that."

"We just don't want to leave our wonderful home," Belle whispered, her voice cracking.

"I know," Dad said, in equal quietness. "I don't want to leave Wildcat Hollow either. But we have to. There is no way we can get around it, except by some miracle."

And so, the kids began praying for a miracle. Every evening before they went to bed, someone prayed for a miracle. Every morning at the breakfast table, someone prayed for a miracle. On the way to and from school, a miracle was prayed for fervently.

But the miracle never came. Two months passed, and nothing happened that resembled a miracle. Dad and Mama were growing less and less intent on praying for the miracle while the kids grew in their impatience to see one happen.

Another family meeting was called near the end of November. The kids sat in the living room again, facing Mama and Dad.

"Well, you all know exactly what we're meeting about," Mama said.

"We're moving anyway, aren't we?" Neena whispered, looking at the floor. "God never gave us a miracle, so we have to move."

"Oh, honey," Mama said, placing her hand on Neena's knee. "God never promised us a miracle. We prayed for one, but He knew what should happen. We will have to move like He wants us to."

"I'm going to miss everyone so much," Mae said, her voice cracking under the weight of her emotions.

"I know," Mama said, wiping a tear. "Me too."

And so they wept, and they cried, and they sobbed in that little house in Wildcat Hollow which was soon to be no longer a Bennett residence.

NINETEEN

THE FIRST WEDDING AND THE MOVE

SPRING of 1943 was one of equal sadness and joy.

Ruby's wedding was approaching rapidly, and she talked more and more about it every day. The wedding was to be held in the barn. Yes, the old barn, with its hayloft and rope swing. That is the place Ruby wished to be married to her beloved.

Mama's baby was born two weeks before the wedding. It was *another* girl, who they named Abigail. The older girls tried their hardest to help Mama with the new baby and the wedding preparations.

In early December, Mama and Dad had chosen where the family was to move. A little community seven miles away, named Bickle's Cove, had good land for farming. Only a few families already lived there. Dad went and bought nearly two hundred acres of land with a little two-room log house in Bickle's Cove. They were to move a week after Ruby's wedding.

The only problem now was the selling of Wildcat Hollow. It was over one hundred and sixty acres, but no one wanted to buy all of it. One small family with two children bought the Bennett's old house that had stood dormant all these years, along with a few acres of land, but the man was a lawyer and the woman was a teacher, so they didn't need the whole property.

No one could be found that wished to buy the remaining acres of land with a small house.

The problem weighed on everyone's hearts until Oswald came to breakfast one morning with the biggest grin upon his face.

"I have found the way to keep the Wildcat Hollow house in our possession while also allowing you all to move to Bickle's Cove."

"How?" Dad asked.

"Lillian and I will buy this house, and the rest of the property, and we will raise our family here," Oswald said.

The kids looked at Mama, and Mama looked at Dad, and Dad looked at Oswald. He burst into laughter.

"Oswald, my boy, I don't know how we have missed it all these months. Of course! It is the perfect idea. Oswald can live here in the farmhouse with Lillian, and that way when we come visit, we will be able to see our lovely old home."

The kids erupted into cheering and Oswald sat in his chair triumphantly.

"This is the perfect solution; the miracle we've been waiting for," Mama said, kissing Oswald on the cheek.

And so it was settled. Lillian was thrilled with the idea, for she had many memories at the Wildcat Hollow House too. Oswald and Dad went down to the courthouse in Pleasant Grove to settle the matter of land ownership, and Oswald was officially the owner of the Wildcat Hollow House the day before Ruby's wedding.

Ruby's older sister, Ellie Gray, and her two daughters visited for the wedding. They slept on the bed in the kitchen because Ellie was pregnant with her third child. The boys, Oswald, Jack, and Leon, slept on the front porch.

The morning of the wedding, the house was a total wreck. Shoes, dresses, bows, ribbons, brushes, and flowers were strewn along the floor of the living room and kitchen. People were tripping over each other in the anticipation and rush to get ready.

"I need my other shoe," Ann shouted, running about the house.

"Where did my ribbon end up?" Chrissa asked, looking underneath the table.

"Someone tell Leon and Jack to come back inside," Mama said from the kitchen where she was finishing up the cake. "They'll ruin their shorts by playing in the dirt like that."

"I'll tell them, Mama," Belle volunteered.

"Why is Bessie taking so long in the bath?" Lou whined. "By the time she gets out the water will be frozen again."

"Mae, how is Abigail?" Mama asked.

Mae, who was rocking the napping baby, whispered, "She's fine."

"Has anyone seen my bouquet?" Ruby asked.

"They're here on the counter, Ruby," Mama shouted from the kitchen.

"Hurry! The preacher will be here with Gilbert soon," Dad said from the bedroom.

"Wendell, stop chewing on your dress or you'll tear holes in it," Ellie scolded. The little girl shrank away from her, who was as much a stranger as a sister.

"The preacher will be here soon," Ruby said in distress.

"Too late, he's already here," Belle said, coming back inside.

Ruby rushed out to meet her groom. He was nicely dressed in a black suit, but he stood gawking at her. She had on Mama's white dress from when she married Dad, and she carried a bouquet of pale yellow lilies that highlighted her green eyes. Her short blonde hair was curled in ringlets that framed her face.

They embraced, and in the happy moment of youthful bliss, they did not notice the preacher. He cleared his throat lightly, and she turned to him.

"Oh, thank you, Mr. Kanili, for performing the wedding ceremony," Ruby said.

"Anything for you, Ruby," Mr. Kanili said.

The rest of the family began trickling out of the house, expressing their excitement of the coming wedding activities. Mama raced to the barn after finishing the cake to make sure everything was in order, and just in time, for the guests began arriving soon.

Gilbert's parents came for the wedding from Missouri, where Gilbert had grown up. Ruby finally met her father-in-law and mother-in-law on her wedding day. The Phillips came also, and after Lillian embraced the bride and gave so many congratulations, she went to sit with her fiancé.

Friends from church and school gradually filled the available seats until everyone had arrived. People chatted and laughed together, enjoying each others' company as they waited for everyone to arrive. They congratulated the bride and groom on their happy day. Then the ceremony began.

It was a beautiful ceremony, sweet and to the point.

Just like Mama's wedding, Ann thought. *There's tons of little kids who are hungry for cake.*

After the first kiss, there was cake and other sweet treats that were passed around to all the guests. The bride and groom danced to the sweet sound of Mr. Kanili's dulcimer, reminding them of the fateful Christmas party that had brought the two souls together.

After everyone had left, the Bennett family stood with the Raslo family, getting acquainted with their new relatives. But soon it was time for the bride to leave her old house to join her beloved.

So many goodbyes were said, mostly because there were so many people to say goodbye to. Mae and Ruby hugged for a long time, each silently crying because she did not want to leave her sister. After hugging Ruby, the rest of the kids showed around the Raslo's the Wildcat Hollow House. It was just Mama and Dad who had to say goodbye.

"Oh, Ruby, I'm so happy for you," Mama said through tears of joy, clasping her daughter's hands. "I hope you and Gilbert will be very happy. I *know* you and Gilbert will be very happy. You will be a wonderful wife."

"Oh, Mama," Ruby said, tearing up. "I don't see how I can learn to be a good wife without you here in Wildcat Hollow to show me."

They burst into tears and clung to each other, wishing it wasn't so, but it was. Dad and Gilbert looked on sadly.

The family lived the next week in tears. Even though it was only seven miles away, Dad doubted there would be much time to visit Wildcat Hollow. They packed their belongings over the course of the week, each one crying at one point or another at the thought of leaving their home.

The table and chairs were packed into the wagon, along with the beds and blankets. Dolls and toys were lovingly wrapped in shawls to be carried to the new house. Daddy's old flag, which had hung by the back door and guarded the little house fervently, was once again taken down, folded, and packed away next to Mama's nice china dishes and Daddy's carved nativity set.

So many fond memories had been made at the Wildcat Hollow House, and the week was filled with wonderful remembrances of their childhood, and how things used to be back then, and adventures they used to have, and silly things they used to fight over.

"Remember the first night we all moved in together?" Belle asked on the night before they moved.

"And I didn't want to share a bed so I slept on the porch," Lou said, laughing.

"I remember that," Mae said.

"That's when I realized how stubborn you are," Neena said, poking Lou playfully.

"I didn't want to share with three other people," Lou said, raising her hands defensively.

"Remember when we first found 'Daniel and the Lion's Den' at the creek?" Ann asked.

"I named it," Neena said proudly.

"And when we built the garden?" Chrissa added.

"You mean, *we* built the garden," Mae said.

The girls laughed.

"Remember when Mama left Dad in charge and we played hide-and-go-seek in the dark?" Lou asked.

Ann remembered the night clearly. *That was the most fun I've ever had.*

There was a moment of silence.

"Remember the pirate ship?" Mae asked, trying to hide the emotion in her voice.

"And how we'd play dolls for hours in the shade of the trees," Chrissa said.

"And I threw so many acorns off of them, I think I planted some trees," Neena said.

The remark got a giggle out of the girls, but it was not enough to quench the sadness.

"Neena, do you remember the first time we went sharecropping?" Belle asked.

"Oh, don't remind me," Neena said, covering her head with her quilt.

"You asked the butler if he was going to church, and then you specifically reminded him that it was not church day," Mae said.

"Remember the pageant?" Lou asked.

"Oh, *that* was a disaster," Mae said, giggling.

Ann laughed. *Maggie and Wilbur forgot the third gift the Wise Men brought Jesus, Frankincense. And then Reuben fell over when we were bowing.*

"Our first Christmas dance was fun," Bessie sniffed.

"I'm going to miss our old barn with its swing," Ann said.

There was a mumble of agreement from the other girls. In the silence of sadness, each one drifted to sleep within the Wildcat Hollow House for the last time.

The morning sun rose and with it when the Bennett family had to say goodbye to their faithful old home and their closest friends.

There was a parade of wagons as all of the Bennetts' friends came to hug them goodbye one last time. Merrilyn and Ann hugged for a long time. Tears were shed as each family left the Wildcat Hollow House.

More tears were shed and hugs were given to the happy couple, Ruby and Gilbert, and the happy couple-to-be, Oswald and Lillian.

And so, the family waved goodbye to their old life, their old friends, and their old house. They climbed into the wagon and disappeared around the mountain.

The End

GLOSSARY

All ages are in relationship to Ann

Daddy - 50 years older

Dad - 44 years older

Mama - 30 years older

Oswald - 9 years older

Mae - 6 years older

Ruby - 6 years older

Lou - 4 years older

Belle - 4 years older

Chrissa - 2 years older

Neena - 1 year older

ANN - BORN in 1931

Bessie - 2 months younger

Jack - 3 years younger

Dell - 6 years younger

Leon - 8 years younger

Abby - 12 years younger

AUTHOR'S NOTE

As you've read this story, you may have wondered what crazy idea I pulled this story from. *Sixteen kids, all living in a tiny house in Arkansas in the 1930s is a stretch of the imagination*, you may have thought. Well, I'm here to tell you that this story is not of my own making. Although I did sprinkle in some fictionalized characters and events, most of this story actually happened. This is the story of how my great-grandmother, Leona Brenner Rozell, grew up.

What? you're probably thinking, but it's true. She grew up in Pleasant Grove, Arkansas, in a community named Wildcat Hollow, before she moved to a community named Bickle's Cove in Mountain View, Arkansas. Her dad really *did* die, and when her mom remarried, Leona really *did* have fifteen full, half, and step-siblings. Most of the events within this story really did happen, and if you don't believe me, you may as well read it from Leona herself.

LEONA'S RECOLLECTIONS

DICTATED BY LEONA ROZELL AND WRITTEN BY
TRUDI PARKER, 1989

Leona was born to Homer and Elsie Brenner at 3 a.m. on May 18, 1931, in Sulphur Springs, Arkansas. It was Daddy's turn to name the baby and he wanted to name her Leon. Mrs. Shelby, a neighbor lady who had been called in to help that night, suggested Leona as a prettier name for a girl, so he agreed. Mama added the first name Rachel from the Bible.

When Leona was 3, they lived at Beaty near Gravette, Arkansas. She had three sisters: Vergie Marie, Katherine Louise, and Edith Caroline, and Mama was expecting another baby. Leona had a doll named "Cobweb Windowlight." Poor Cobweb Windowlight got left out in the rain one night, and she was never the same. Her face was all wrinkled and cracked, but Leona still loved her.

When Caroline was 5 and Leona was 3, they went to the store at Beaty by themselves and bought green suckers. They were probably two for a penny, and green was their favorite kind. They walked back home under the pine trees.

The family went to Sunday school and church at Liberty Hill Schoolhouse where a lady in a green dress played the piano. The four little girls got stars for perfect attendance there. One Sunday afternoon, they went to the "Daniel in the Lion's Den." That was what Mama called the spring she discovered that came out from the rocks under a bluff. It was a good place for picnics, with a creek where the kids could wade and eat lunch under the trees. They went there with some people from Sunday school and made pink ice cream. The stuff for ice cream was in 3 one-gallon pails. They sat them in a tub of cracked ice and turned them back and forth until the ice cream was frozen. Leona had pink strawberry ice cream, probably for the first time in her life.

When Daddy (Homer Brenner) wasn't working in his garden, he liked to hang out at Hanna's Store or the Masonic Lodge Hall, both of which were nearby. He liked to sit on the porch, smoke his pipe, and talk with the men. When he came home for lunch, which was usually soup, Mama would say, "Slurp, slurp, and back to the store he went." He had a joke that he told about the Masonic Lodge. "This woman kept asking her husband what was the secret password, and, of course, he couldn't tell her. But one night they were eating supper and she asked the secret word. He said, 'Beans and cabbage,' meaning for her to pass them to him, but she thought that was the password. She sang out, 'Beans and cabbage, I'll have you killed. Beans and cabbage, I'll have you killed.'" That was Daddy's joke.

Daddy had a team of horses he used to plow the garden. He got sick the year Leona was 3. It must have been some kind of heart failure. They called it Bright's disease and dropsy. Fluid would collect in his legs. They would swell twice their size and the skin would burst and drain. He did not go to a hospital. He sat in his chair with his feet in a container that came up to his knees, called a lard stand, that caught the excess fluid. Leona remembers Mama telling her to be quiet around Daddy. He passed away February 11, 1934 and was buried at the Beaty Cemetery near Gravette.

The Masonic Lodge held a funeral service that included music and Taps with a gunfire salute. Leona remembers a long line of people walking out to the cemetery, especially one man who had lost his legs. She saw how neatly they folded the flag that was draped over the casket and gave it to Mama. The flag was always at the different places they lived, including the Hollow. Leona doesn't know what became of it after that. When Daddy died, he left Mama, who was pregnant with John Homer, and the four girls: Vergie-9, Louise-7, Caroline-5, and Leona-3.

After Daddy's death, it was decided that Mama and the children would go live near Grandma Lavinia Hughes. She and John Coombes (Mama's dad) had divorced years before, and she was now married to William Hughes. They lived in Newark, Arkansas, with their daughter, 13-year-old Evelina. But before the family could move, they must wait until the baby came.

Mama's Aunt Ida and Uncle Charlie Coombes came to stay to help get things settled and help them move. Their teenage boys, Pete and Sherman, came and stayed awhile. They loved to pester Leona. They would pitch her doll, Cobweb Windowlight, back and forth between them just out of her reach. They would go upstairs and tell Leona to look up. When she did, they would spit in her face. If she ran upstairs to get them back, they would slide down the banister.

The Morgans were their neighbors. Helen Morgan remained Vergie's friend even after they moved several times. They would write letters to one another. The team of horses was sold to Mr. Morgan. He and Uncle Charlie were going to load the horses on a truck to take them away. They backed the truck up to a steep railroad embankment and were leading the horses in one at a time. They got the first one in, but he was scared. He began to rear and pitch. He fell out of the truck. His neck was broken, and he died. They were successful in getting the other one in and hauled away. Leona would never forget that poor dead animal, lying there on the ground, so soon after Daddy had gone too.

When the baby, John Homer, was about 3 months old, they loaded all the household goods on Mr. Morgan's big truck. Mama's Uncle Charlie came along to help. He, Vergie, Louise, and Caroline rode topside. Mr. Morgan drove. Mama, Leona, and John Homer rode in the cab with him. They started off for the 100 mile trip to

Newark. They probably followed old Highway 62 through Eureka Springs. They stopped at a service station along the way to use the restroom and change the baby's diaper. It was the first time Leona had seen a big white commode or real toilet tissue. At home, they went to the outhouse and used pages from old catalogs.

They camped at a little spring and park for the night. Mama had packed a basket with fried chicken, potato salad, and other good things. For breakfast the next morning, they had bologna and store-bought bread. In those days, it didn't come already sliced. They managed to get it sliced with Uncle Charlie's pocket knife.

That morning, they were at the river crossing at North Fork. They had to call the ferry man from the other side. This took a long time, and it was foggy and cold. John Homer was crying with the colic. Leona felt like crying too. It was so cold and damp that you could hardly see anything.

It was after dark that night when they arrived at Grandma and Granddad Hughes' place. Granddad had hung a lighted lantern on the gate post so Mr. Morgan could find the way. Waiting to greet them were Grandma and Granddad and their 13-year-old Evelina (who had beautiful long, red hair that hung in curls). Also waiting were Grandma's married daughter, Bonnie, her husband, Johnny Brumley, and their children, 2-year-old Willie Lea and 3-month-old Johnny Dee. It was the first time in about 12 years that Mama had seen her mother, sister, and half-sister.

Grandma gave them some supper and made pallets for them to sleep on that night. The next morning they went to their little house about a mile away and unloaded everything, including the chickens. They had been cooped up so long, they were happy to be fed and to scratch in the dirt.

Grandma and Granddad lived on one of 'Boss' Allen's sharecrop farms, where they raised cotton and cattle. 'Boss' Allen seemed happy to have a hard-working widow with 5 kids. He provided the little house for them, gave them pick sacks, and told them to "Pick it clean. Don't leave any goose locks." Vergie, Louise, and Caroline went to school and Mama picked cotton for 'Boss' Allen. Mama would let John Homer ride on the pick sack and Leona stayed at the end of the rows. There was another little girl who stayed there too. One time she had some soda crackers and gave Leona one big cracker, which was 4 together. That's the way they came then. Leona had never tasted them before.

They were happy there despite the hard work. They had a good home, a barn with a cow named Dolly and her calf. They had chickens and ducks, and a black and white dog named Jack. Marma had put up a lot of hay in the barn loft for old Dolly. It was Johnson grass that she had cut with a hoe. John Brumley and Mama's sister, Bonnie Brumley, lived a few miles away. John used to say that Mama could put up more hay with a gooseneck hoe than he could with a mowing machine. The girls had fun with the hay. The loft was full and spilling out on the ground. They would climb the ladder to the top and slide down the haystack to the ground.

Mama said that Leona could write and spell her name when she was two years old, but she doesn't remember doing that. The first birthday she remembers was when she was four. Mama made her a little dress out of a flowered material with a matching bonnet and bloomers. It had tiny orange and yellow flowers with green leaves. She put it on and she and Caroline walked over to Grandma and Granddad Hughes' house.

They had a garden with popcorn and peanuts. Mama would roast the peanuts and set the pan way up on top of the cupboard until the girls got home from school, then they could have them for a snack. The others liked to laugh about the things Leona said or did. The garden was fertilized with cow manure. Once, she saw some tumble-bugs rolling balls. She ran in and told Mama that "bugs were rolling away the potatoes." They had a big laugh out of that. There was no radio or entertainment.

They would all recall funny times such as when Caroline and Leona went over to Grandma's. She told them that on the way she "saw a 'pider' and got a stick to kill it but it was done already dead."

When they got to Grandma's, she was churning butter. Grandma was real shaky. (She must have had Parkinson's disease.) When the butter was done, she gave the kids some on cornbread. They thought it was a real treat.

Grandma's daughter, Evelina, said, "Come out to the barn, Leona, I want to show you something." They went to the barn. It was all dark and dusty. Evelina went up to the rafters and told Leona to look at a barrel that was there. When she looked, up popped a scary black "ghost" out of the barrel. It scared her so bad, she cried, and Evelina just laughed and laughed. Then they went home and had cake. Mama always made a cake for Leona's birthday.

Mama's sister, Bonnie, and her husband, John Brumley, lived about five miles away. John came in his wagon and took the whole family home with him at Christmas. They spent two or three nights there. John's family had a big house near them. His mother, father and some of his brothers and their children were there. Santa came and handed out gifts and candy to everyone. When they returned home, Santa had been there too. Leona got a little toy horse on wheels to pull around. The other girls got small china dolls and headbands. There was lots of Christmas candy too.

Santa had some helpers in Kansas City, Kansas. Before his death, Daddy had some favorite nieces, the four daughters of Uncle Ulyses Brenner, his older brother. They were Geneva, Mary, Alice, and Edith. After Daddy's death, they did not forget their poor little cousins in Arkansas. Nearly every Christmas, they sent gifts. Many kept in touch for years. When Leona was in high school, Mary still sent money and gifts which were very much appreciated. Daddy hadn't felt the same toward his other brothers, Charles and Otto Brenner. The girls never saw their uncles or their Brenner grand-parents. When Daddy finally received his part of his mother's estate in 1929, ten years after her death, it was a check for $4.37. He tore it up and blamed Charles for it being such a small amount. He said he would never speak to him again, but when they knew he was dying in 1934, Charles and Otto both came and made peace with him, but "Liss" and his four daughters were always his favorites.

That Christmas Eve at the Brumley's, Aunt Bonnie had held both Johnny Dee and John Homer, and let them both nurse, because she had extra milk. A few weeks after Christmas, word came that Johnny Dee had taken pneumonia and died. Poor Aunt Bonnie and Uncle John, they still had Willie Lea, and they were to have four more daughters, but no more sons. When the family gathered for the funeral, Leona saw the tiny pink casket of their baby cousin. It was very sad, but this was not the end of sorrows. Granddad Hughes' oldest son, Russ, lost a little two year old boy with infantile paralysis. The mother was in bed with a newborn baby when he died. The families gathered for this funeral also. Leona saw little Ray laid out in a white dress trimmed in lace. He looked so small, even to her, who was only three at the time.

The older girls were going to school and Leona was so happy to see them come home on those cold winter evenings. She would run and tell them what was cooking for supper. A lot of the time, it was whippoorwill peas and cornbread, but sometimes when Jack, the dog, had caught a rabbit, there would be meat and gravy. Sometimes there would be roasted peanuts or popcorn for an after-supper treat. Of course, Dolly, the cow, gave them all the milk and butter they could use and they had eggs from the chickens and ducks.

Early in the spring of 1935, they received word from Granddad Hughes and Boss Allen that both the Black and White Rivers were at flood stage and they must prepare for a flood. They should take Dolly, the cow, and her calf to high ground and put the chickens and ducks in the smokehouse so they could fly up in the rafters. If it looked like it would get too high, they would come for them in a boat. The house was about four feet off the ground. By morning, water was lapping at the floor of the porch, but the girls had fun. The older ones tucked up their dresses and walked around the yard carrying the younger ones. Granddad Hughes came to see how they were and brought several big catfish that he had caught because of the high water. As the water receded, it left puddles that bred mosquitos. Soon, all the children were coming down with malaria, chills and fever. Vergie was the worst. She would talk nonsense when her fever got high. Mama called it "talking out of her head". She decided it was time to get the doctor. He gave them all quinine (very bitter white powder), calomel, and Grover's chill tonic. Quinine was very hard for little kids to take. Mama would mix it in hot chocolate or put it in a baked sweet potato. Calomel came in tablets, but Grover's chill tonic was a grainy liquid that had to be taken by the big tablespoon full.

When Leona and the other children were sick, they liked to hear about the "olden days". Mam told them that when the Cherokee Strip opened up for homesteading in 1898 or '99, the Pritchards came from Steel, Missouri. The Coombes came from Indiana. John Coombes and Lavinia Pritchard met and married in Oklahoma before it became a state. They had their first child, Ada, about 1900. Elsie Mae (Mama) was born November 26, 1901. Then came Alvin, Calvin, and Nellie. When Lavinia was pregnant with Bonnie, she and John Coombes were divorced. Ada had died in the big flu epidemic. This left Mama as the oldest child.

"Tige" Prichard and his cousin, Taylor Frane, went from Oklahoma to Stone County, Arkansas. Their mothers, who were both widows by this time, lived in Stone County, Arkansas. Then Lavinia, who was pregnant with Bonnie, also went to Stone County. She met and married Williams Hughes there. William Hughes had three grown children, John, Sadie, and Russ. Mama's uncle "Tige" married Sadie.

When Lavinia and John Coombes divorced, Mama was the oldest. She was about twelve. She had to stay with her father to help take care of the younger children. At about age sixteen, she left and went to Tulsa, Oklahoma, to get a job. She found work there as a waitress. At age 21 she came to visit the family who had moved to Stone County. In January of 1922, Mama married Homer Brenner in Joplin, Missouri. Mama told them that at the time they married, she was 21 and he was 42. He worked in the oil field. They lived in

Kansas when the first two children, Vergie and Louise, were born. They lived in Arkansas when the others were born.

When Mama's uncle Tige heard that all the kids were sick with chills and fever from living in the "bottoms", she urged Mama to move to the mountains. It was the 160 acres that he had homesteaded when he moved to Stone County, three miles from Pleasant Grove, Arkansas. Mama could have it for $100. Most of the land was rocks and mountains, but there was a little creek running through the center of the place with some farmland on each side. Uncle Tige had moved up the mountain to a place with a larger house. Someone else was in the little house in the hollow at the time, but it was urgent that Mama and the kids get out of the lowlands. So they all moved in with Uncle Tige, until the little house would be vacant. As it turned out they stayed there several months. They had cousins to play with. There was Bobbie, Joe, Elsie, and Drewhy. They later had a girl, Mearl Ruth. Vergie, Louise, and Caroline went to school at Irons Point with the two oldest kids. Their teacher was Anson Siler. Aunt Sadie had more than she could handle before Mama and family got there, but Mama always worked hard, so she helped with cooking, gardening and laundry. One time, Elsie and Leona got stuck in some mud and got their hightop shoes and long stockings all muddy. Somebody had to clean up that mess. Aunt Sadie had clean white sheets and soft feather beds. Mama, Leona, and baby John Homer were sleeping upstairs when the roof just above them caught fire. Mama threw some water on it from the inside and Uncle Tige got on the roof and someone handed up buckets of water. It wasn't much of a fire but he had to patch the roof.

Finally, the day came when they moved to the little house in Wildcat Hollow. Mama and the kids just walked down the mountain. There was no trail, but Mama knew the way they needed to walk until they came to the spring and creek. Then they just followed the creek until they came to the little house. Someone had gone around another way and brought over their household goods in a wagon. They went to work setting up the cookstove and table and chair in the kitchen and the heater and beds in the other room. Besides the two large rooms, there was a small room off the porch. The porch had a banister around it and Mama planted a seven sisters red rose (bloomed in clusters of seven) that climbed up to the roof. There were some built-in shelves in the kitchen and up on a high shelf, Mama found a little willow basket that someone had made and she said it was for Leona, who kept it for a long time. There was a barn across the creek for old Dolly and her calf, the chickens, and the ducks. They walked on stepping stones to cross over. In the winter, they could get their water from the creek, but in the summer, the creek dried up and the water must be carried from a spring about a quarter of a mile up the hollow.

It was early spring and Mama wanted to make a garden. Mama hoped that she could get Bob Davis, the closest neighbor, to plow up the ground. It wasn't long after they moved that the peach trees started to bloom. There were at least five trees in the yard near the house and a lot behind the house. This was called the orchard. Showers of pink petals would fall off the trees and Leona would gather them in her little basket. It was just like a fairyland. Mama took some pictures. One was John Homer peeking over a peach limb, playing peek-a-boo.

The girls were still having health problems. Mama went to the store in Pleasant Grove. She got medicine and food. By then, the government had started giving Commodities such as prunes, oatmeal, cocoa, meal, and flour. They had canned food, potatoes, and sweet potatoes. She still put that bitter quinine in the hot cocoa and the baked sweet potato. It wasn't long until they had ripe peaches and fresh food from the garden. Mama peeled and canned lots of peaches in half gallon jars. She also canned green beans and English peas. Early in the spring, they picked wild greens (poke, dock, mouse ear, wild beet, lambs quarter, dandelion, and wild onions). Many old people in the south talk about eating "poke salat" much the same as in Wildcat Hollow. They had sassafras tea and spice brush tea. These were supposed to be good tonic for them. Catnip tea was especially good for babies who had colic. Other herbs were used as medicine: horehound was good for sore throat; wormfuge was for parasites in the digestive tract.

Vergie, Louise and Caroline started school at Arbana, where George Noricks was the teacher. His parents ran the post office at Kahoka. Arbana was later consolidated with Mountain View. One day while the girls were at school and Mama had gone to the spring to get water, Leona, age five, and John Homer, age two, were alone. A man named Albert Scott came to visit. The children were not afraid of strangers in those days. He asked them, "Where is your mother?" When they told him, he went to meet her and helped carry the pails of water back to the house. They sat and talked a while, and he bounced John Homer on his knees. He told them his wife, Savana, had passed away and that he had seven kids. The oldest girl was married and the oldest boy was away at CCC camp. That left five at home. Later, they found out that it was his married daughter, Ibura, who had lived there before them. Albert Scott came for one more visit, then he and Mama went to Mountain View and were married. They went in his wagon pulled by his mules named Kate and Jane. When they came back in a couple of days, the wagon was loaded with household goods and five kids plus a cow being led behind and a dog named Fido. They had left old Jack with Granddad Hughes.

Now, each one of Mama's girls had a twin. Vergie had Manilla (age 11), Louise had Ruth (age 9), and Caroline had Maudie (age 7). Leona's twin was Betty (age 5). John Homer was two and Albert's boy, Wesley, was fourteen. He had polio when he was young and walked with a limp. They called Albert "Dad". That's what his kids called him. Dad had Wesley to help him with the milking and caring for the mules. The big girls helped Mama with the little kids and housework. Dad and Mama planted cotton, corn and sorghum cane. It was called Texas Seeded Ribbon Cane because its seeds are planted and not the stalks as in real Ribbon Cane. They also had a big patch of peanuts, a big garden with popcorn, beans, peas, cabbage, carrots, onions, beets, potatoes, sweet potatoes, radishes, and turnips.

Mama and Dad cut timber and made enough shingles to cover the house. Then they made pickets, enough to fence in the garden and yard. Cattle, hogs, and goats had free range. That means they fenced in the crops but the animals were free to graze in the woods and mountains. Mama and Dad built a new chicken house and a pig pen, where they fattened out several hogs. Then the next year they got a herd of eight goats. Soon they started raising little goats. Dad made a shelter and a pen for them. Leona loved those baby goats. The little kids would get in the pen with the kids (baby goats). Leona would turn a feed bucket over to sit on and let the goats suck on her fingers. They tried goat milk but nobody liked it. They had plenty of cows' milk anyway.

They had hogs that ran free, too, but they would keep a couple penned up to butcher for meat when they got fat enough. When they wanted the hogs to come home, they would call, "Pig, pig, sowee", and the pigs would come running to the nice hog trough that Dad had made for them. When it was time to milk the cows, someone had to go down the cow trail and drive them back to the barn with a big stick. Dad usually did the milking and Mama strained it and put it in the lard buckets in the cellar. They had built a cellar with shelves for canned food. Mama always canned in half-gallon jars. It was a cool place for the milk. When the cream came to the top, she would skim it, and after enough was saved, and it was sour, she would churn it in the old butter churn. It had a dasher that she splashed up and down until butter came. She would put the butter in a clear glass bowl. They could have buttermilk and cornbread and have butter with their biscuits in the morning. Mama and Dad built a big chicken house with a row of nests on one side and roosts on the other. They had plenty of eggs to eat. When a hen "went setting", Mama would save the best eggs, about a dozen, and make pencil marks on them. These went under the setting hen. Then if another hen laid an egg in her nest, you could tell which eggs were fresh. About 21 days later the little chicks would hatch, but not all at once. Mama would gather them in her apron and put them in a box behind the old wood cookstove. The hen would stay on the nest until all the eggs were hatched. Mama then would put all the little chicks and the hen in the chicken pen. The hen would call all the chicks to her and spread her wings over them to keep them safe.

Mama and Dad both worked in the timber. Besides the shingles for the roof and pickets for the fence, they made bolts. These were blocks of wood that were the right length for barrel staves. Mama and Dad cut the tree down with a crosscut saw, and the big girls helped saw the log into blocks that had to be split into quarters. Dad did most of the splitting. He used a sledgehammer and wedges. They were loaded on the wagon and taken to a sawmill where they got paid for the bolts.

Mama canned vegetables such as English peas, green beans, tomatoes, pickles, sauerkraut, and corn. When peanuts were ready, they were pulled and put in the dry shed. Onions, potatoes, dry beans, and peas were also stored there. Corn was put up to make meal for cornbread, grits, or mush. The sorghum cane made molasses. When the leaves started getting dry on the cane stalks, the big kids went down the rows cutting off the leaves. Then someone cut the cane stalks and loaded them on the wagon. They took them down to a place by the "Big Gate" where the Molasses Man was setting up his mill and cooking pan. Then the mules were hitched to a long pole that stuck out from the mill. As the team walked around in a circle, someone fed the cane into the mill and the juice ran into a tub that had been put into place. When enough juice was in the tub, it was poured in the molasses cooking pan. The man had lit a fire under the pan. The juice was poured into the first section of the pan which was divided into at least three sections. As the man was cooking juice in the first section, the team was still grinding out juice, so the first section would be stirred and emptied into the next section to make room for the fresh juice. Then when it was in the third section, it must cook until it was just right to be molasses syrup. This was poured into the syrup buckets of one gallon, half-gallon, or quart sizes. Molasses making was done in the fall.

That winter, they had the first Christmas together with the "whole bunch". Mama always got a cedar tree. Dad nailed some crossed boards on the bottom to make it stand up. They had their old decorations - crepe paper streamers and those bells made of paper that open, Christmas roping they used every year and glass balls that were from Vergie's first Christmas. They also made popcorn strings for the tree and roasted peanuts on the old pot-bellied stove for snacks. They had to go to sleep early because Santa Claus wouldn't come until they were asleep. If he caught you not sleeping, he would throw red pepper in your eyes, and you would get a bundle of sticks under the tree instead of presents. The little kids hung stockings and the next morning, each one would have an apple and orange. There would be a couple of coconuts and some peppermint sticks under the tree and the hard candy that came in ribbons and pillows. Mama made lots of cookies, pies and cakes. For meat, there would be ham or some other hog meat. All the Christmas' they had there were about the same. The rich Brenner cousins still sent packages at Christmas. One Christmas they got a mandolin, a mink stole, and a little girls' fur coat that fit Caroline, so she got to wear it. None of them knew how to play the mandolin, but it was very pretty. The back was like a potato bug with stripes and the front had mother-of-pearl butterflies.

When it was time to butcher the hog that had been penned, it was stuck with a knife to let out as much blood as possible. After that, the hog would be put in a barrel of hot water. This loosened the hair so it could be easily scraped off. When this was done, it was hung up and cut open, saving the parts that were useful: liver, heart, leaf fat and a few others. Then the meat was cut into hams, bacon, shoulder, and ribs. Some parts were for sausage and mincemeat. This mincemeat was canned in jars and used to make mince pie. The tenderloin was fried right away and was the best part of the day. The other larger parts were pickled in a barrel in a solution of salt water. Salt was stirred in a tub of water until it had enough salt to float an egg. Some saltpeter was added. This tub of solution was poured over the hams and other parts in a barrel, covered and left for a certain amount of days. Then, the parts were removed from the solution, rinsed off and hung up, usually in a smokehouse, but at that time, they did not have one so they coated the meat with a molasses and pepper mix and it was cured enough to last as long as needed, but it tasted too salty.

Later, after they got the goats, Dad had to butcher them when the family needed meat and money. He had to bleed them to make the meat good, so he hung them by the hind legs and cut their throat with a really sharp butcher knife. It only took one stroke of the knife to make the cut. The kids always said they couldn't stand to watch, but there was a really big, dead log close to the place where goat butchering was done. They would get behind the big log and try not to look. It was so awful, they had to peek and then wished they hadn't. He skinned the goat, cut it up into roast, ribs and other stuff. Then he would wrap it in clean white cloths and take it down the road to sell. They had some of it fried and some made into ground meat. They did not make barbecue or chili. Mama didn't know about casserole dishes. She cooked meat in gravy in a pressure cooker. Also, rabbit and squirrel were cooked this way.

After crops were "laid by" the whole family went to a white sandy beach on the White River. Dad would hitch up old Kate and Jane to the wagon, load up camping stuff and they would go to their favorite camp spot on the White River. The kids played in the white sand and swam. Dad and some of the older kids fished. Mama tried to keep a fire going and cook for all the gang. She had her Brownie camera and took pictures of them and of Dad and the boys if they caught a big fish. If they caught enough, it was fish for supper -- if not, it was potatoes, gravy and biscuits made in a Dutch over coals. Mama had baked some cakes, pies and cookies to bring along. There was a spring there but no one liked to drink the water. It tasted something like Epsom salts. Mama said it would probably work the same way too. They also had canned stuff like tomatoes, green beans, sauerkraut, and peaches. They had pancakes for breakfast. Mama had to make a lot of pancakes cooked over an open fire to fill up all the kids. They had butter and molasses syrup on them. They had fun, but then it was back to their little house in Wildcat Hollow.

When they came back, they went through "town", Pleasant Grove. They didn't buy anything, but they got to see the two stores and the ESSO gas pumps and the Coca Cola sign. There were no nickels for them to get pop. It would have taken too many for all of them, so Dad and Mama drove their wagon load of kids and camping stuff right on through town and across the creek and on up toward the hollow. Theirs was the last house. Dad put old Kate and Jane back in the pasture and they dragged all the quilts and camping stuff back to the house. Then it was back to gathering crops before school started in September.

Leona and Betty started school when they were six. During the summer, Mama had made all four sets of "twins" new dresses. She had a treadle sewing machine that she got when she first left home at age sixteen. Dad made a new trail up the mountain to school. It was shorter than the old way. Leona and Betty shared a lunch pail together and they fussed over who had to carry it most. It was a big syrup pail and Mama and Vergie made the lunches. They put some fried potatoes in the bottom and two forks to eat them with, then two biscuits with meat and two with butter and syrup. Sometimes they had a biscuit with fried egg.

On Leona's first day of school at the Arbana one-room school-house, the teacher was a man named George Noricks. When they walked up to the school for the first day, the teacher was sweeping the steps and said, "Good morning". Leona was afraid to say anything. She already knew how to read and count. They were seated with boys on one side and girls on the other. Each desk was for two kids. Leona sat with Earlene Tuttle. Mr. Noricks asked each of the small kids to come up to his desk. He had given out the books as they were seated. Leona's was called a primer. When it was her turn to read for the teacher, she took her primer up to his desk. He opened it to the first story and pointed out words with his pocket comb. When she was done, she took her book and almost got his comb with it. He said,

"Don't try to steal my comb." She was so scared and embarrassed she ran back to her seat and wanted to cry. They went home on the new trail Dad had made up the mountain. It went through a tight place between rocks at the first bluff. At the second bluff, the trail was pretty good but off to the right was a spring coming out of an overhang of rocks. That was a nice place for them to go and get a drink and get their feet wet in the water on a hot day.

This was about the time that Mama and Dad got a new baby, Wanda Mae Scott. Then a year or two later there was Leonard Franklin Scott. The house was soon filled with teenage girls. Mama and Dad let them have parties and young men who knew how to play guitars, fiddles and mandolins came. The girls could not have dances except square dances and dancing games like "Skip to My Lou" and others. Dad could keep time to the music and call the games. Mama and Dad both had funny songs they sang when there was no one to play music. Dad had this funny song he sang about the "Darby Sheep": the biggest sheep that was ever fed on hay. Mama liked to sing "Mr. Grumbler": he did say he could do more work in a day than his wife could do in three. Dad sang "The Cat Came Back": gave him to a man going up in a balloon, said, give him to the man on the moon but the cat came back, the cat came back the very next day cause he couldn't stay away any longer.

A few years had passed and Manilla (the one Vergie's age) met a man at the parties and they gave permission for her to marry Odell Bounds. He had a little shack as all the houses were. It was up on a mountain a few miles from their home, and after awhile the little girls could go visit. Betty and Leona spent the night and Manilla knew how to cook and bake biscuits, so they enjoyed their stay. Afterward, they walked back home. Later on, Manilla had a baby boy and they all went in the wagon to see them and the new baby named Jerry Bounds.

Still, later Odell Bounds, the husband, went into the army and so did a lot of others they knew. It was the beginning of World War II. Many young men who had never been out of the hills and hollows were drafted into the Army and many never came back. The war started the year Leona was ten (1941). They heard about it at school from the teacher, Tollie Leonard. During the time he was there at Arbana School, he liked to make up war songs. Part of one was to the tune of "Darling Nellie Gray": Yes old Hitler, you are doomed, the Allies are on the boom and you'll not be Germany's ruler anymore. Old Tito (Japan's ruler) will be riding on a rail, whey they get through with Old Tojo (Italy's ruler) there'll be no one to tell the tale.

The war song Leona liked best was "There's a Star-Spangled Banner":

There's a Star Spangled banner waving somewhere in a distant land so many miles away. Only God's great heroes get to go there, where I also wish to live someday. There is Lincoln, Washington, and Perry, Nathan Hale and Collin Kelly too. There's a Star Spangled banner waving somewhere, waving o'er the Land of Heroes brave and true.

Not long after that, Arbana school was closed and they went to Pleasant Grove School for a while. Then in 1943 they moved to Bickles Cove.

ACKNOWLEDGMENTS

First, I want to thank my God, who blessed me with the time, energy, and support I needed to write this book.

I want to thank my beta readers and launch team, who helped me edit and publish this book and encouraged me along the way. Without them, I'd still be on draft four.

A huge thanks goes to my wonderful cover artist, Rhiannon Youngvall, who labored tirelessly over the picture and learned how to format Amazon covers with me.

Another huge thank you belongs to Jenna Petty, who edited this book.

My family deserves the biggest thanks I can give. Their support and guidance through this journey has been invaluable.

I want to thank my grandmother, Ma, who found countless family pictures and records to help me keep everything and *everyone* straight.

I also want to thank Vergie Brenner Forrester (one of the real sisters!) and her daughter, Judy Weeks, who talked with me through many letters about what their life really was like.

And, she didn't want me to thank her, but a thank you goes to my writing mentor, Julien Jamar, who answered my endless questions and taught me the beauty of pursuing my dreams.

Words can not describe what these people mean to me.

ABOUT THE AUTHOR

Aria Stubblefield, or Ari D., is a senior in high school and a published author of the duology *The Hollow* and The Cove. She began writing this series during the COVID-19 shutdown in the spring of 2020. Her great-grandmother, Leona, always wanted her childhood to be turned into a children's story, and Aria was more than happy to embark on that adventure. She is grateful that her first published books honored her great-grandmother.

Besides writing, she loves singing in her choir, dancing, and acting. When she graduates high school, she plans on getting her master's in counseling psychology so she can get her license in counseling. She is incredibly thankful to everyone who has helped her as she published both of her books.

Made in the USA
Columbia, SC
07 November 2021